# THE LOCKSMITH'S LAMENT

# MIKE WHITTAKER

# WHITTAKER

---

# THE LOCKSMITH'S LAMENT

Acknowledgements:

To Clare for helping me stay grounded

To Cooper for encouraging me

And to Asher Penn for expertise and advice and your example.

# THE KEY

The first sensation that engulfs you when you find yourself in a foreign bedroom is the olfactory assault. The occupants, familiar with their own fragrances, remain blissfully unaware. But Gil, every time he ventured into an alien sleeping chamber, was acutely aware of the cocktail of odors. It was, to him, an occupational hazard — a byproduct of a life dedicated to secrecy and stealth. He understood the truth of particulate nature; that the noxious emissions, like an acrid fart, disseminated into the very air he breathed, carrying with them minuscule fragments of their origin. Gil often pondered the remarkable journey of these fecal particles, traversing layers of fabric, sheet, duvet, and cover, only to reach his nostrils mere moments after evacuation. It confounded and repulsed him.

Clad entirely in black, from his slip-on sneakers to his balaclava and black latex gloves, Gil surveyed the darkened room. His non-reflective blue-blocker sunglasses offered a modicum of assistance, enhancing what little ambient light was available. These lenses were a mere step below night-vision goggles—a necessity for his profession, ensuring the absence of clues, fingerprints, DNA, and, most importantly, witnesses.

The couple in the bed lay cocooned in the sanctuary of deep slumber, their consciences unburdened by guilt. Gil knew the concealed wall safe was to his left, hidden discreetly behind a hanging mirror. He was equally aware that women possessed a lighter slumber than men; the slightest sound or disturbance could awaken her. He gingerly removed his sneakers and approached the woman's side of the bed.

From his satchel, he extracted a small vial of clear liquid. Removing the stopper, he squeezed the rubber bulb, allowing the liquid to fill a glass tube. A gentle release deposited the contents onto the woman's pillow. The ether was promptly absorbed by the fabric, and for a fleeting moment, the woman stirred. Her eyes fluttered open, her head rose slightly, only to be met by a sharp inhalation. The ether worked its magic swiftly; her head dropped back onto the pillow, her breath deepening. A thin rivulet of drool trickled from the corner of her mouth.

Gil replicated the procedure on the man's side of the bed, who remained undisturbed. Gil had anticipated no interference from the sleeping couple. He now turned his attention to the mirror and the concealed safe.

With meticulous care, Gil cleared a space on the vanity large enough to accommodate his satchel. He secured the ether, tightened the cap, and returned it to the bag. He lifted the mirror off its hook and set it beside the vanity. The wall safe was now exposed. From the satchel, he withdrew an aerosol can and released a fine mist into the safe's recess. Brilliant red lines materialized in a three-by-three grid, visible within the dissipating mist. Gil knew they were there, and he had come prepared. He extracted a peculiar contraption from his bag, an amalgamation resembling a colander and a disco mirror-ball, to the uninitiated.

Another spray of mist, and the red lines became apparent. Gil positioned the mirrors on the cavity's lip and gave it one more spray. The red lines, reflecting from point A to alternate point B, were now part of an unchanged, connecting circuit. The alarm system remained unaltered. Gil was accustomed to these maneuvers.

Continuing his operation, he retrieved a small box attached to a two-inch-wide flexible jumper cable. The wall safe was digital, a common modern lock, although Gil preferred the old analog variety. With the right gadget, unlocking these digital locks was a straightforward task, especially the one before him. It always puzzled Gil how wealthier individuals seemed to skimp on the purchase of their first safe. He suspected that after tonight's encounter, the owner might consider investing in an upgrade. Locking the barn after the horse ran off, or some such parable ran through his mind.

Gil located the interface on the number pad and plugged in his device. It powered on, embarking on the task of decrypting the combination. A small window, cycling through twelve-character spaces, accomplished the task in just sixty seconds. The combination was revealed to be a mere six characters in length. As the door swung open, an abrupt snort emanated from the bed behind him. Gil froze. Another snort, and he swiftly disconnected the lock breaker, coiled the cable, and stowed it in his bag. He turned slowly to find the husband sitting up in bed.

Immersed in darkness, Gil couldn't discern the man's face, but he sensed that the man wasn't gazing in his direction. The man flung the covers off, swung his legs over the bed's edge, and pivoted, positioning his back toward Gil. The effect of the ether was apparent as he staggered. The man shuffled through the dim room, exiting the bedroom and progressing down the hallway to the bathroom.

The click of the bathroom door reached Gil's ears, followed by a faint stream of light spilling into the bedroom along the hall. He listened to the sound of the man urinating, accentuated by two loud farts that, were it not for the ether, might have disturbed the wife's slumber. In the subdued light, Gil discerned that she remained asleep. Gil stayed frozen in time.

The bathroom light extinguished, the door swung open, and the man returned to bed. Within moments, his rhythmic breathing resumed, and Gil realized he'd been holding his own breath. He released it, quietly, retrieved the ether from his satchel, and deposited two more droppers' worth on the man's pillow. Hopefully, that would suffice. Gil returned to his task.

The interior of the safe, a one-foot cube, concealed three small shelves on the right side and an open space on the left. Three bundles of hundred-dollar bills were liberated and tucked into his satchel. Two passports, original marriage certificates, and wills were casually left on the vanity, along with a prenuptial agreement.

At the back of the safe, on the open side, rested the object of his pursuit, that which he'd been commissioned to retrieve. The bundles of cash served as delicious extras, but the ultimate prize occupied a tiny plastic case no larger than three square inches. A black obsidian key lay on red velvet, encased within the transparent plexiglass. Gil enveloped the case in a cloth from his satchel, ensuring the delicate key remained unscathed. His client insisted on its pristine condition.

Satisfied that the key was secure, he conducted a final survey of the safe, discovering nothing else of value or annoyance. Gil packed his gear, ensuring no harm could befall the key, and re-shod himself.

He positioned himself in the bedroom doorway, grappling with an old, familiar temptation. It was an impulse he wasn't proud of — a hunger that often gnawed at him after a job well executed. The break-in was elementary; locating the safe and unraveling its combination, a thrilling feat. Yet, compared to the overpowering urge that seized him at this juncture, those achievements paled. It wasn't the first time he had wrestled with this compulsion.

Gil crept back to the woman's side of the bed. This time, this one time he was determined to put dollar signs and duty before his compulsion. The obsession is still there, he just doesn't have to act on it. **He strained in the dark** to see that she was still asleep. A beautiful and desirable woman, and vulnerable, she was exactly his kink. He knew it was time to leave. This was how you got caught. He pulled the covers back over her shoulder. He made his way to the door and out of the house.

He felt like an idiot. As clever as he might be when it came to thievery and safe cracking, he had one weakness: helpless women. He wasn't into BDSM, didn't ask lovers to let him tie them up, nor did he like to force anyone, but he did like them subdued in other ways. He knew he was sick.

Once he was outside the house, he walked the three blocks to where his van was parked in an alleyway behind another beautiful house. As he made his way, he took off the various accoutrements of his profession, the balaclava and gloves, and unzipped his jacket revealing a t-shirt beneath. Just a local out for a late-night/early-morning walk. Nothing to see here, move along. Not that there was anyone to see him at this hour.

The neighborhood was deserted. A couple of living room windows gave off a faint blue haze of people watching TV. The streets were clear. At his ride he opened the side panel and dropped his satchel inside. He unzipped it and took out the plastic case with the key. He put that in his pants pocket for safe keeping. He slid the door closed with care so as not to wake anyone in the neighborhood. He looked back the way he came and thought about the woman again. I'll be sleeping with my hands on top of the covers tonight, he mused.

# THE SUNRISE TAVERN

His full name, Gil Tyrannus, resonated with a
ruthlessness matched only by his insatiable
determination. He didn't suffer fools, he wasted no time,
and showed little regard for the collateral damage left in
his wake. The world had offered its chances, nearly
destroying him, but now it was the age of Gil Tyrannus,
and his demands were paramount.

Every visit to the Sunrise Tavern brought Gil face to face
with its unyielding scent. He pondered the power of
smell, how it could dictate his mood. In the Sunrise, it
was a relentless assault on the senses – a cacophony of
stale beer, mingled with urine, body odor, and cigarette
smoke. Even at two in the afternoon, the bar teemed with
lowlifes and predators. Paradoxically, this seedy
environment was where Gil felt most secure, among
those who thrived in the shadows – thieves, losers, and
addicts.

The Sunrise was an establishment that opened early,
devoid of any social conscience. Its owners cared only
for the meager profits from beer sales and room rentals
above. The clientele, if one could dignify them with that
title, consisted of welfare grifters, down-on-their-luck
prostitutes, and the occasional working man seeking
solace in a buzz. No one belonged here, but in the end,

this place owned them. The Sunrise was the final refuge of ambitions and hopes that had withered and died, oblivious to their own fate.

As Gil approached the bar, he noticed a peculiar figure out of place. A man in a suit sat at a solitary table, sipping coffee. Gil couldn't fathom anyone drinking coffee at the Sunrise. The rest of the tables were adorned with glasses of cheap draft beer. This anomaly piqued his interest, and he kept a watchful eye on the well-dressed stranger.

The sticky floor beneath him didn't invite contemplation. Gil couldn't help but wonder about the source of the stickiness. It was bad enough if it were just beer, but this place was infamous for frequent brawls and under-the-table hand jobs, making the thought of what his shoes had been exposed to even more unsettling. Every visit to the Sunrise tempted him to buy a new pair of shoes.

A few faces acknowledged his presence with forlorn smiles. Among them was Marty, an old acquaintance from a past collaboration. But Marty was now a shadow of his former self, consumed by addiction and age. Gil felt a twinge of pity for the trembling old man but swiftly reminded himself of Marty's uselessness.

Seated at the bar, Stan, a mountain of a man, was the healthiest-looking person in the establishment. However, appearances were deceptive; Stan was quick and lethal when provoked, making Gil vigilant during their interactions. Stan was not a man to be crossed, as Gil had witnessed during an incident involving the disposal of a body.

Stan was engaged in a phone call when Gil arrived. Gil overheard the tail end of the conversation. "Yeah, he's here now, sir." A pause, absorbing information. "I'll tell him." Stan, with his meaty finger, signaled for Gil to hold off any questions. When the call concluded, Stan pocketed his phone and beckoned Gil to sit beside him.

"Got the thing?" Stan asked, a hint of urgency in his voice.

Gil reached into his jacket and produced the small plastic case, containing the obsidian key. He extended it towards Stan, who displayed the palm of his hand, indicating Gil should hold onto it. Stan said, "He wants to see you this time."

Frowning, Gil responded, "That wasn't the deal. I hand you the key. I do not meet the guy." Stan glared at Gil. "I never meet any of the clients."

Stan's demeanor remained implacable. Without meeting Gil's eyes, he delivered a stern verdict, "You'll meet him this time. He's willing to pay double. He wants to see you in person."

Stan's unexpected change of the deal unsettled Gil. He had his reservations about the meeting and questioned Stan's motives. Why would Stan willingly let himself be bypassed in the deal? Suspicion gnawed at Gil, and he turned to leave, emphatically rejecting the offer.

As Gil departed, he tossed back a half-hearted, "Tough luck," leaving Stan to deal with his disgruntled client.

Under the afternoon sun filtering into the bar, Gil's annoyance simmered. He had lost a potential commission for the key and couldn't understand the sudden change in the client's terms. Gil was a man who trusted no one easily, and his instincts rarely failed him.

Gil made his way outside. He was halfway up the block when the suited man who had been in the bar called to him from the curb, gesturing towards a black car. Gil paused and watched the man.

"My boss wants to see you," the stranger announced, making it clear that a simple refusal wasn't an option. The concealed bulk of a hefty firearm underscored his authority. He held the front passenger door open and waited.

In that moment, an assortment of thoughts raced through Gil's mind. His physical fitness, and martial arts expertise played out in his mind. He knew he could inflict harm, if necessary, but the prospect of a one-way trip held his curiosity. Besides, Stan's promise of double the payment lingered enticingly in the air.

Gil took a step forward toward the car, when from off to the side, at the entrance to the Tavern, Marty called out, "Gil! Long time."

With an air of defiance, Gil stepped past the suited man and walked over to Marty. "I thought that was you."

"You weren't going to say Hi, kiddo?" Marty said with a sad smile.

"You know me, in and out." Gil shot a look at the driver. Back to Marty he said, "You know this clown?"

"I've seen him before. You should go." Marty looked like crap.

Gil asked, "You need anything."

"Could use a couple of bucks."

Gil reached into his pocket and gave him two one-hundred-dollar bills. Marty was shocked. This was about a hundred and ninety more than he expected Gil to part with. "Thanks kiddo." Gil maintained eye contact and his grip on the bills tightened, until Marty realized there was something more than the dollar bills being handed to him. Gil had palmed the small plastic case into the folded bills. When it dawned on Marty that Gil was trusting him with a secret, a tear formed.

"Stay safe partner. I won't charge you any VIG on this. I'll get it back next time we meet."

Marty's expression never wavered. "Yeah, kiddo. You bet." He pocketed the bills and the case containing the obsidian key. As far as the driver was concerned, they had been discussing interest on the two hundred dollars.

Still in defiance mode, Gil opened the rear-passenger-side door and reposed in the car's back seat. He grabbed a bottle of water, relaxed into the plush seats, and closed his eyes. The driver slammed both doors and got in the other side. Gil's thoughts swirled, focusing on Marty and the key.

His recollection drifted back to the day he first met Marty, nearly two decades ago.

## **MARTY**

When Gil reached the age of sixteen, he made the audacious decision to sever his ties with his parents and abandon formal education. School was no longer for him, and he opted to apprentice with a locksmith. He proved a swift learner, driven by an insatiable hunger for knowledge. Gil devoured trade journals and studied every user guide he could get his hands on, delving deep into the intricacies of locks and safes. For three years, he honed his skills under the tutelage of the master locksmith, and by the time he turned nineteen, he was a virtuoso in cracking tumblers, combinations, and even the latest fingerprint-based security systems. There was nothing Gil couldn't breach.

Word of Gil's prodigious talents spread like wildfire, a boon for his burgeoning enterprise. He expanded, hiring three employees, then three more a year later, and another three after another half a year. His stock portfolio grew in tandem with his burgeoning reputation and ego. His future seemed secure; his success guaranteed.

Then, the stock market plunged into a maelstrom. The companies Gil had invested in, misled by their deceptive reports, transformed into bottomless financial abysses. He had to let his employees go, sell off three of his four trucks, and desperately seek to refinance his struggling business. The banks clung to the remnants of their resources, the government bailing out corporate behemoths while the little guys like him received nothing. He felt cursed by an unseen hand.

Gil lost everything: his storefront, his business, and ultimately, his solvency and spirit. In this darkest hour, suicide seemed a plausible option. But salvation, or perhaps something more sinister, awaited in the form of Marty.

On a frigid winter night, Gil parked his truck behind the Sunrise Tavern after closing hours. He easily tapped into the bar's electrical grid to power the truck's heater, unable to rest with a sense of unease hanging over him.

He intended to find a safer spot to sleep once the night ebbed away, when it was warmer, and he wouldn't need to steal electricity.

As Gil huddled in his truck, he heard a faint noise from outside, a gentle tap on the panel door. "Go away!" he bellowed, "I've got a gun!" His voice reverberated within the truck, but the tap persisted.

Gil's nerves flared, and he seized a socket wrench from his toolbox, not prone to violence but ready to defend himself if needed. He unfastened the lock, threw the latch, and kicked the door open, aiming for the element of surprise and disarmament.

The truck's interior light spilled into the inky alley. Gil couldn't discern much outside, the darkness enveloping all. Cold air streamed in, and he watched his breath cloud before him. "Who the hell is out there?" Gil shouted, realizing he was trapped if the intruder possessed a weapon. He held the wrench aloft, preparing to ward off an attack, and leaped out into the obscurity of the alley.

A figure in a hooded jacket stood near the truck, his elbow resting on the side panel. It took a moment for Gil's eyes to adjust. The man smiled, raising his empty hands in a placating gesture. Gil lowered the wrench but held it visibly between them.

"Are you the locksmith?" the man inquired.

Gil remained cautious and inclined his head toward the side of his truck, the vibrant logo announcing, "THE LOCKSMITH." It bore his name, phone number, and address, with the 'O' and 'C' forming a lock. Beneath, in smaller script, it read: Gil T. Proprietor. "Might be. Who's asking?"

Marty reached for a handshake and introduced himself. "My name is Marty. If you're the guy I think you are, I might have a job for you. Do you need a job, kiddo?"

Gil, harboring thoughts of working for sustenance, took the man's hand. "I'm Gil."

"I know," Marty said, nodding toward the truck's inscription. "I've been looking for you. You had quite the reputation before the world blew up." He waved his hands, indicating the entire planet.

"You know me?" Gil inquired.

"Know of you, more like it, kiddo. Come on, let's find a place for some coffee. You got gas in this thing?" Marty claimed the passenger seat with mock enthusiasm.

Gil was momentarily stunned. Could this be the break he had silently prayed for? He secured the panel door, placed the wrench behind the passenger seat, and started the truck.

They drove in silence, eventually locating an all-night café. Marty bought coffee for both and a muffin for Gil, and they sat inside the truck's cab in the café's parking lot, engaging in a lengthy conversation that continued until the sun was high in the sky.

Marty divulged that his livelihood depended on commissions from a very particular patron, and a select group of clients—bankers, art dealers, and mobsters. These commissions flowed through a portly man named Stan, a part-owner of the Sunrise Tavern. Their work was diverse, spanning from infiltrating store windows to living rooms, with the occasional safe-cracking mission thrown into the mix.

"Why me?" Gil inquired.

"Why not you, kiddo?" Marty retorted. "You want in, or don't you? I need someone who's ready to make some sacrifices to get ahead. I've got two jobs that need a set of skills like yours. Takes a few days to complete. If you don't like it, you walk away. No hard feelings."

Gil mulled it over, reflecting on his current dire circumstances. "I'm in," he finally said, shaking Marty's hand on it.

Marty's relief was palpable. He handed Gil two fifty-dollar bills. "Head over to the City Center Motel on Main, get a room, clean up, and rest. Meet me at the Sunrise this afternoon, at four o'clock. If I'm not there, wait for me. If you see a big man at the bar, that's Stan. Don't approach him if I'm not around. Understand?"

Gil nodded, understanding the instructions. "Motel, clean up, meet at Sunrise around four."

"At four," Marty stressed, sternly.

"At four," repeated Gil.

Marty teased with a cryptic clue about the first job: "It's bloody."

"What do you mean?" Gil inquired.

"We're stealing blood," Marty said with a smirk. "Think about that. Get out of here, see you at the bar."

Later that afternoon, just before four, Gil arrived at the Sunrise Tavern. The ground outside was dusted with snow, and his boots left tracks as he stamped his feet upon entry. All heads turned as he entered, except for a portly man seated at the far end of the bar—must be Stan. Gil chose a table near the front and waved away the waiter. He waited. At five past four, the door swung open, and Marty walked in.

Marty made straight for Stan. He looked around the room as he did, but didn't see Gil seated in the dark corner near the door. His eyes hadn't adjusted to the gloomy interior. Marty and Stan shook hands, and Marty took the stool next to the big man. Their heads leaned toward each other in quiet conversation, they were too far away for Gil to make out what was being said. He stood up and walked toward the two men. As he got closer, he could make out individual words. When he got close enough to make out complete sentences, the two men stopped talking and they turned their attention to him.

Gil felt awkward and out of place and time. He was destitute, desperate and dependent on a stranger's good graces. Stan didn't look friendly, at all. He was big, meaty. There was a couple of days growth of beard on his face and his hair was uncombed. Stan jabbed Marty with his elbow, he flinched and spoke "Hey kiddo, you made it." Marty got up off the stool. "Come meet Stan the man."

Stan was already looking in the opposite direction at a man coming at him from the back of the bar. Marty grabbed Gil by the upper arm and led him to an empty table a few feet away, "Let's wait this out."

A heated conversation ensued. Stan's voice grew louder, punctuated by several "yeahs." What Gil could make out, was that the man had paid an amount to Stan for some kind of product and Stan was holding out on him. The situation escalated, and the man became increasingly threatening. Stan argued that the man owed him from a previous debt and was withholding his payment from this transaction. The man vehemently disputed the arrangement, and things took a violent turn.

In a single, fluid motion, Stan's colossal fist connected with the man's face, the ensuing impact causing an audible crack as the back of the man's head struck the floor.

Turning to Marty, Stan ordered, "Get this piece of shit out of here."

Marty still had a firm grip on Gil's arm and, when he rose, he brought Gil along. Together, they lifted the unconscious man from the floor. Marty inquired, "Where do you want him, Stan?"

"Get him the hell out of here. Use your imagination," the burly man replied, his attention on a racing form by now.

Carrying the lifeless man with Gil at the head and Marty at the feet, they maneuvered around tables and exited through the back door, depositing the fallen man into the alley. Gil checked for a pulse at the man's throat.

"Anything?" Marty inquired.

"Yeah, but it's weak. This guy needs an ambulance," Gil replied.

Marty promptly walked back into the bar. As he stood in the open doorway, he said to Gil, "So? Call one and be done with it, or don't, and come back inside. Won't make a difference. Dead today, or the next time he crosses Stan." With that, he returned to the tavern.

After a full sixty second interval, Marty appeared at the door to the Sunrise, again. "What the hell are you doing,

Gil?" Gil stood over the unconscious body at his feet and only stared back at Marty.

"Look, kiddo. I'm only going to say this once. If you want to make money, the kind of money that will get your ass out of the hole for good, do the thing that needs doing and do it now. Here's what you're giving up by dilly-dallying." Marty pulled a roll of hundred-dollar-bills, bound tightly by a pink elastic band, from his pocket. He held it out to Gil. When Gil reached for the money, Marty put it back into his own pocket. "Nah, kiddo. You have to earn this, and you haven't shown me you have what it takes." With that, Marty returned to the warm, somehow inviting interior of the tavern.

Gil's mind raced. He considered the body on the ground before him. The unconscious man wore an insulated jacket over a sweatshirt and jeans. Gil found himself conflicted, unsure of the right course of action. Then, something dark and cold seemed to take hold of him. A shadow passed over the alley. Gil immediately braced himself. It was as if a switch had been flipped, plunging him into a shadowy abyss of indifference. He walked to a nearby dumpster, opened the lid, and peered inside. There was ample room, with a few garbage bags to keep the man company and shield him from the cold. Gil heaved the body into the dumpster, slammed the lid shut, and left him there to his own devices. To hell with him.

Gil returned to the Sunrise Tavern, ready to meet his new employer and uncover the secrets behind the enigmatic "bloody" job. Stan, a giant of a man with a penetrating gaze, scrutinized him with the precision of a carnival worker guessing weight. He extended a meaty hand, and they shook on their agreement. "You ready to make some sacrifices? That's what working here is all about. Sacrifice." Stan and Marty shared a side-long glance.

Marty added, "That's what we're all about, here, sacrifice and reward."

Gil nodded his assent. "Yeah, whatever you need."

Smiling at the younger man, Stan made known the tavern's two unwavering rules, pointing to a sign on the back wall:

Rule 1: The boss is always right.

Rule 2: When the boss is wrong, see Rule 1.

And thus, Gil found himself entangled in a world of intrigue, where locks and secrets held equal value in the shadows. "Think you can follow those rules, yeah?" Stan's voice, a low, gravelly whisper, carried an air of unmistakable authority. He didn't wait for a response, merely releasing Gil's hand as if their meeting was but a mere formality.

Stan settled back onto the stool, swiveling toward the counter with a practiced ease. "Marty, yeah? Take him out and get him working. You're going to make some money, kid."

Gil couldn't help himself. The words fell from his mouth of their own volition, "How much money?"

Stan's monstrous rage erupted and Gil took a step back. "What you think, this is a fucking job interview? Get this kid out of here and get him to work."

The unspoken contract between them was cemented as Marty dragged Gil behind him. Together, they left the dimly lit confines of the Sunrise.

"You almost blew it, kiddo. Don't ask stupid questions." Then he stopped on the sidewalk and corrected himself. "Better yet. Don't ask any questions, with the stress on the any".

Gil felt unfairly reprimanded, but he moved on. There was money to be made, after all.

His truck remained where he had parked it, a faithful sentinel in the twilight. As they embarked on their mission, day gave way to night. Streetlights flickered to life, traffic faded, and the city retreated into a slumber. The truck eased into the shadow of a looming billboard, its headlights extinguished, and the engine silenced. The passenger window cracked just an inch, a precaution against fogging. In the frigid silence, they waited, hidden in the darkness for twenty eternal minutes. Not a single car passed in either direction. The interior of the vehicle mirrored the chill of the night outside.

When the appointed time arrived, they disembarked from the truck. Gil carried a satchel by its sturdy canvas handles, the weight within barely noticeable. Together, they crossed the deserted street, the distant barking of a dog providing the only punctuation to the stillness of the night.

As they reached the corner of the building, Gil paused to drop his bag and rub his hands vigorously to chase away the cold's persistent grip. Marty, better prepared for the elements with his insulated gloves, offered a whispered tip. "Stick your hands in your armpits, kiddo. They warm up faster that way." Gil complied, providing brief respite from the biting cold.

With questions nagging at his thoughts, Gil finally voiced one. "So, this is a blood bank?" Marty acknowledged with a nod. "And the guy we're robbing this place for just wants his own blood back."

Marty nodded once more, his voice carrying the weight of their peculiar mission. "Close, kiddo. We're after a rare blood type. Our benefactor wants it and we're going to get it. The damn place is holding onto it, claiming they need it more than he does."

Gil, always curious, pushed further. "Marty, that only makes sense. Why would he want something they need?"

Marty's response was swift and resolute. "Because he's rich, and he justifies himself to no one, not even us. Let's get going."

Leaving no room for further inquiry, Marty guided Gil down the alley toward the blood bank's unassuming back door. They stopped and crouched in the shadow of a neglected dumpster, as the first snowflakes began to fall. Their exhaled breaths, visible in the frigid air, were the only signs of life.

"Alright, kiddo," Marty began, outlining the complex operation ahead, "there are six or seven stages to get through in this place. There's a guard keeping an eye on the video cameras, and there's a god-damn alarm system. You got everything you need to pull this off?" He presented the job's parameters, punctuating each point with a raised finger, scrutinizing Gil's face for acknowledgment. Gil nodded, and Marty produced a small walkie-talkie, which elicited a responding click from the matching device in Gil's pocket.

Marty's parting words were brief but brimming with purpose. "Let me know when I need to come back."

With that, Marty patted Gil's shoulder before retracing his steps up the alley, returning to the safety and relative comfort of the truck. Gil was left alone, and the weight of their brazen undertaking hung heavy in the frigid alley.

Unfazed by solitude, Gil's keen eye scanned the alley and the building's rear. He counted three cameras pointed at the blood bank's back door. Intuitively, he surmised that if he could trace all three cables to a single junction box, their mission would be significantly simplified. Carefully, he tracked the cables to their entry point on the building's exterior, confirming that all three converged at that junction box. However, it was perched some thirty feet above, unreachable from their current vantage point. The fire escape fell short of their reach, and the building's five-story height loomed ominously. Marty had given him a rough plan and equipped him with almost all of the tools needed for this challenge.

Gil ran back to the truck. Marty was reclined in the passenger seat, hat tilted over his eyes, breathing deeply. Gil opened the rear door and extracted his collapsible step ladder. He grabbed that and retrieved his satchel of tools as he jogged back into the alleyway.

The night unfolded as a blur for Gil, an adrenaline-fueled rush where memory waned, replaced by the sheer intensity of the moment. He recalled scaling the fire escape from the dumpster. He expanded the step ladder to its maximum length. He stood upon the top step of the ladder, the one emblazoned with the bright red warning: NOT A STEP, then connecting his own camera to the junction box, providing a discreet view of the alley and back door to the guard inside the building. Two clicks on his walkie-talkie signaled Marty, and their mission advanced.

Gil descended from the fire escape just as Marty arrived back on the scene. Gil handed his partner the satchel while he ran the step ladder back to the truck. Marty stood holding the bag gingerly, by the handle, as a nineteen-fifties husband might do while the wife tried on some dresses. Gil relieved him of the satchel and jogged past the older man.

Gil's nimble lock-picking skills granted them entry through the back door, the first of several locked barriers. A second lock separated them from within the stairwell to the blood bank's inner sanctum. However, there were more cameras to contend with, and at this juncture, the night's harrowing details loomed large in his mind. These were the memories he wished to forget, but they had become inseparable from his new life—a transformation ignited when he had thrown that man into a dumpster.

Marty had advocated subduing the guard to eliminate the need for additional tech gadgets, and despite his reservations, Gil had merely uttered, "You're the boss." And so, they found themselves here.

The video room lay in the basement, another layer of locks barricading their path. Gil's lock-picking prowess was their key, granting them access to the hallway outside the guardroom. In the pitch-black interior, the gleam of several video screens cast an eerie glow.

Cautiously, Gil inched toward the video room's entrance, ajar and propped open to dispel the heat generated by the monitors. His balaclava concealed his face, and when Marty noticed, he donned one too. Marty, ever vigilant, crawled behind Gil like a guardian.

With sudden swiftness, Gil stood and entered the video room, delivering a precise strike to the guard's head. She crumpled without a fight, and Gil checked her pulse to ensure he hadn't inadvertently ended a life. She was still alive, breathing, and he heaved a sigh of relief. He retreated momentarily to retrieve silver duct tape from his satchel, returning to secure her, lest she awaken during their covert operation.

Then he went to her feet. She was wearing a mid-length, black skirt and pantyhose. As he duct-taped her ankles together he ran his hand along the smooth length of her calf. Gil saw from the corner of his eye that Marty was still occupied searching for the video storage. He allowed his hand to roam up under the hem of her skirt. He felt a rush of excitement as he did this. He'd always been a good guy, an honest tradesman and he thought, respectful of women. He felt a twinge of guilt as he stroked the woman's leg, but he couldn't stop. He felt compelled to continue.

From behind him Marty said, "Bingo. Found it kiddo." Gil stopped fondling the woman and turned her over onto her stomach and duct-taped her hands at the wrist, behind her back. He plastered a small patch over her mouth. She looked so helpless lying on the floor, like that. He jumped a bit when she moaned and started moving on the floor. When she regained full consciousness, she started screaming into the duct-tape. It wasn't loud enough to carry out of the room, but she was terrified.

Marty pivoted and knelt beside the woman's face, adopting a tone that both calmed and intimidated. "Darling, hush now. We mean you no harm. We'll be in and out within a mere twenty or thirty minutes. Take a nap if you like, we couldn't care less." The woman's sobbing softened, though muffled by the stubborn duct tape. Tears streamed from her eyes, forming delicate pools upon the floor. Marty turned back to the task at hand.

With a deft touch, he depressed a concealed button on the hard drive, linked to the security system. Two trays slid open, revealing a pair of compact discs. Gil swiftly pocketed them. While the monitors still displayed live camera feeds, their images were no longer being recorded. They now held absolute control.

Ensuring their captive remained securely bound, Marty and Gil ascended to the second floor, where the coveted blood stores awaited. Gil's skills came into play once more as he manipulated locks, granting access to a hidden stairwell door and the blood storeroom's main entrance. Their mission hinged on penetrating a colossal walk-in freezer adjacent to the blood storeroom.

The walk-in chamber, illuminated from within, featured glass-doored, floor-to-ceiling shelving units. These held hundreds of bags of blood, suspended from gleaming chrome hooks. The left wall bore labels denoting the various blood types: A, AB, B with a + or - designation, while the right wall bore the simple label "O," outnumbering all others. All the cabinets were securely sealed.

Marty consulted a note concealed within his jacket pocket and shared their elusive target with Gil. "Here, we're in search of a true treasure, my friend. A literal pot of gold." Marty scanned the room, eventually discovering the object of their desire on a single shelf within a glass unit. A white label clearly read "RHnull," and six small blood bags dangled from hooks. "This is it. We've found it."

Marty signaled for Gil to work his lock-picking magic, a task accomplished with the ease of a seasoned pro. "Easier than cracking a can of beans," Gil quipped.

Stepping inside, Marty collected the blood bags in a makeshift cloth bag he had unfurled from his back pocket. "Our mission is complete, kiddo. Let's go."

Gil packed away his assortment of tools, including his trusty picks, into his satchel. By the time he finished, Marty had already made his way to the exit door that led to the dimly lit alleyway. Gil called out to him, "Hold on, Marty. I just need a minute to see the lady is alright."

As Gil brushed past Marty on the way down to the basement, Marty stood impatiently at the exit. "What's the holdup, kiddo?"

Handing Marty his satchel on the fly, Gil replied, "Could you take this to the truck for me? I'll be quick."

"You need any help?"

"No, thanks. One man operation."

Marty exhaled in exasperation. "For God's sake, hurry it up."

Gil made his way to the video room. He stopped at the doorway. The woman was as they'd left her, face down and trussed like a calf at a rodeo. She must have been struggling to get out of the duct tape. Her jacket was askew and her blouse was half untucked from her skirt, exposing the side of her now naked waist. And her skirt had ridden up her thighs more than it was designed to be worn. There was a snag in her pantyhose that caused a run up her leg from her ankle to just above her knees.

This was the sexiest thing he had ever seen. The switch that was toggled earlier today when he tossed that man into the dumpster closed another circuit for him, now. He could do whatever he wanted, right here, right now. The devil had him in thrall. And she couldn't stop him. Gil's boot scuffed the edge of the doorway. The woman turned her frightened face at the sound. Wide-eyed and tear stained face, Gil thought she looked radiant. He stepped into the room. Maybe she saw something in the way he was looking at her, but she started screaming through the duct tape, again. Somehow, that only stoked the fire in Gil's brain.

"Shh, shh, relax. I'm not going to hurt you."

Gil knelt down and began stroking the woman's hair, trying to calm her. She started crying and twisting her head away from his hand. Gil ran his hand down her shoulder and caressed her back. The woman started twisting her body to avoid his hands. Gil was getting annoyed. "Fucking, stop," he said. Gil lifted his balaclava and snugged it at his forehead, exposing his face. He smiled and tried to calm her.

The woman screamed at him. She tried to kick him with no effect due to being taped at the ankles. But she was able to knee him in the side. Gil laughed. He pulled her jacket backwards and that left her shoulder bare. The woman's scream was muffled by the tape. He pulled the jacket harder and both her jacket and blouse were pulled down to expose her upper arm and her bra-covered breast. Gil was fully aroused. His breath came in ragged gasps. He was out of control. He wanted release.

Gil reached into the woman's brassiere and grabbed her by the breast. He squeezed it. The woman struggled to get free. She was crying and screaming. He released her breast. Her skirt had now ridden all the way up over her buttocks, and new snags ran all the way up both legs of her stockings. She wore black, thong panties under the hose. Gil reached into her pantyhose and stroked her ass. The woman let out a whine, a mewling cry that let Gil know she was helpless against him. His fingers touched her between the legs. She clenched her thighs in an attempt to fight him off.

"You better not leave any fucking DNA, kiddo," Marty's voice came from the doorway. Gil tore his hand out of the woman's panties and pulled his balaclava back over his face. He stood to confront his partner.

The woman heaved great sobs. Her crying came out as muffled pleas. She tried to catch Marty's eye, thinking him a saviour. He ignored her. Speaking to Gil, he said, "You have a lot to learn, kiddo. If you want to succeed at this game, you leave nothing behind. No DNA, no prints and if you're seen, no witnesses." Marty pulled a gun out of the waistband at the small of his back and fired two shots into the woman's head. The blasts were deafening in the enclosed space.

Gil scrambled backwards until he hit the computer console. He pressed his palms to both ears, "Holy fuck, Marty. What did you do?"

"Saved you from yourself, is what I did. What the fuck were you going to do?"

Gil was incredulous, "I wasn't going to kill her," he shouted.

"No, you were going to leave evidence, or prints or something behind that would get you caught, that would probably get me caught, too. You weren't thinking. I had to do the thinking for you. With this," he waved the gun in Gil's face. Marty put the gun back into his trousers at the small of his back.

"But, Jesus, Marty. She's fucking dead." Gil's
expressions and movements were exaggerated by shock.
He staggered around the room.

"Yeah, kiddo, and it's all your fault. 'One man
operation' my ass. If you'd come straight out when we
got what we wanted, we'd be gone by now. But, no. You
want to play slap and tickle," and he stressed the next
words, "with a witness." Marty grabbed Gil by the
shoulder and turned him to look at the body on the floor.
He said, "She wasn't yours to play with. Don't be so
goddammed stupid." Marty looked around the place. He
said, "You leave anything else lying around?"

"No. I didn't" Gil whispered this like a child being
punished for a misdemeanour.

"Good. Let's go," Marty declared with a steely resolve.
As Gil hesitated, the weight in Marty's voice grew,
"Now. We leave now. I'm not fooling around here." Gil
complied, leading Marty up a dimly lit staircase and out
to the waiting truck. The early-morning air was frigid,
and their surroundings devoid of any other vehicles. A
thin shroud of snow had draped the silent streets. The
only traces they might leave behind were the tire tracks
from Gil's truck and their own footprints, but Marty had
a contingency in mind for that as well.

From the depths of Gil's truck, Marty retrieved two hefty
whisk brooms, each weighed down by cinder blocks.
The rear door of the vehicle swung open, and he directed
Gil to drive away. Then, with the brooms extended to the

width of the truck's tires, Marty allowed the substantial cinder blocks to erase any telltale signs in their wake. After they had traversed three blocks and merged onto a busier thoroughfare, he retracted the brooms and secured the rear doors.

Marty clambered from the back of the truck into the passenger seat and cast a searching gaze at Gil before delivering a grim ultimatum, "Try something like that again on a job with me, and I'll make sure a bullet finds its way into your skull."

Pausing at a red traffic light, Gil glanced back at Marty. Though there was no overt confrontation in his eyes, the remorse was unmistakable. He nodded in agreement, muttering, "Sorry, Marty."

Marty leaned back in his seat, regarding Gil for a moment before he spoke, "I'm not saying don't indulge your whims. Just don't let them spill over into a job with me. If you want to get yourself caught, fine, go for it. But don't drag me into it."

Gil's voice wavered as he pleaded, "I couldn't help it, man. I've never felt that way before. It was like something took control."

Marty retorted wryly, "Yeah. The devil made you do it," and they shared a laugh, a strange mix of adrenaline and exhaustion punctuating the moment.

As the laughter subsided, Gil grew serious, "Maybe it was. I don't know. Remember this afternoon, when I tossed that guy in the dumpster for Stan? Something, a feeling, came over me, and I just didn't want to deal with it. So, I tossed him." The pair rode in contemplative silence. "I've never done anything like that with the guard. It just had me, and I couldn't stop."

Resting his cheek against the frigid window, Marty spoke gravely, "I've seen it happen before. That's how people get caught. You've got to get a grip on it before it gets a grip on you." Silence dominated the rest of their journey until Gil dropped Marty off at his destination.

Gil spoke softly, "Thanks, Marty."

Marty quizzically responded, "Thanks for what?"

Gil kept his gaze fixed forward, his fear of Marty's judgment keeping him from meeting the older man's eyes. He whispered, "For looking out for me."

After a brief pause, Marty responded with a hint of paternal reassurance, "No problem, kiddo. It might not be the last time. Go home and get some sleep."

Before Marty could shut the door, Gil leaned over and asked hurriedly, "What does the guy want with blood?"

Marty took his time, his hand on the doorframe, "I don't know. What do you do with blood?" He shut the truck door before Gil could reply, leaving Gil to watch him until he reached his front door, then drove away.

Gil's thoughts weighed heavily as he contemplated his transformation: "Two days ago, I was a destitute locksmith. Today, I'm an attempted rapist and an accessory to murder. Just fantastic." He switched on the radio and headed toward the City Center Motel. **He needed to masturbate as soon as he got back.**

In the shadowy intersection of their lives, their partnership solidified after that initial job, the alliance of Gil and Marty grew stronger, the boundaries between legality and outlawry blurred in the storm of their collaboration.

Marty, the wily mentor, imparted to Gil the various tricks of his trade, a clandestine apprenticeship where rules were woven on the fly. The first rule they agreed upon: Gil refrained from direct sexual or violent acts, shielding Marty from culpability. And the second rule: Marty swore off any gratuitous bloodshed, ensuring Gil's deniability. Gil, however, drew the line at arming himself, rejecting a life as a killer, while Marty held a chivalrous commitment to sparing the fairer sex.

It was their final operation that led Gil to understand the worrying depths of Marty's predicament at the Sunrise. Together, they robbed a notorious biker gang's headquarters in the distant valley, a place infested with vice, and mayhem long before they infiltrated. It marked their final collaboration, an unwitting twist that entangled them in the labyrinth of drug trade. Marty's clandestine pact, unbeknownst to Gil, opting for product over cash, thrust both partners into the murky world of narcotics. Gil's principles remained steadfast; he could endure assault and murder but refused to be ensnared by drug dealing, a perilous endeavor destined to attract numerous and various law enforcement hounds.

Situated in a bankrupted restaurant miles away from the city, the gang's stronghold nestled in a popular bedroom community. Their bold heist required meticulous reconnaissance. Three months of patient observation paved the way for their scheme, designed by Gil to infiltrate the den and exit with ease. Famous last words, of course.

Once a month, the bikers congregated for drug-fuelled parties in the ground floor's main chamber. Yet it was the basement, the infernal crucible where money and drugs mixed, that was their focus.

In the past, 'stepping' referred to the art of diluting narcotics, an ingenious method to extend their supply and multiply their profits. These days, they adulterated with fentanyl, cheaper and deadlier.

Amidst the blaring music and anarchy that flooded the neighborhood, two neophyte guards flanked the club's entrance, protecting the bikers' prized possessions, fifty-plus Harley Davidson motorcycles in the parking lot. The rear, however, remained vulnerable, housing the apparatus that kept the partying hordes oblivious to their impending doom.

A truck, positioned in the alley, fifty feet beyond the Harley parking lot, its engine rumbling beneath the noise, a shadow concealed in matte black paint. The company insignia obliterated; it was the linchpin of a clever plan. A two-inch fire hose unfurled from the truck, soon to become an instrument of death.

The guards, stationed outside, remained ignorant of the clandestine machinations behind the clubhouse. One, absorbed in a joint and the pursuit of a teenage girl's favor, neglected his duty. He followed the young woman back toward the parking lot, oblivious to the two men and their truck in the alley.

The rear of the building contained the infrastructure for keeping the clubhouse comfortable. There was a massive central-air-conditioning unit taking up most of the space behind the building. Inside the main room there were several vents with little strips of cloth flying out from them, showing that air was moving. No one paid any attention to this. No one cared about the little strips of cloth, just so long as the air-conditioning kept working.

The rear of the building, meanwhile, concealed the partner's dark secret – the fire hose lead from the end of the truck's exhaust pipe, to the colossal air-conditioning unit and was churning out carbon monoxide. Its voluminous intake was sealed with a mass of duct tape.

Carbon monoxide, an imperceptible assassin, unfurled its tendrils within the raucous party, a creeping threat overlooked amid the drug-induced stupor. Marty, tapping the gas pedal within the truck, maintained the deadly dance, while Gil observed with bated breath. Hidden from the world, Gil's old locksmith truck proved its worth once more.

Silent in his preparations, Marty checked his weapon, a Glock 17, loaded with thirty-round clips and equipped with a silencer. With a nod from Gil, a silent query, Marty's reply was succinct. Tonight, they were both aware of the necessity of lethal intervention. Yet Gil's question lingered: did Marty have a plan for the guards outside?

Marty, his balaclava concealing all but his eyes, replied cryptically, leaving no room for doubt, "One-man operation, kiddo." A shared chuckle hinted at the gallows humor born from their numerous escapades.

As Marty glanced at the tachometer, Gil confirmed that their time had come. The relentless music masked the impending disaster, drawing Gil's nod of consent. Marty deftly loaded a magazine into the weapon, the metallic clack echoing in the dimly lit truck cabin. He pocketed another two clips, his eyes filled with a steely determination. "I've got ninety rounds with me. I'm only going to need two of them, if it all works out," he whispered. In the soft glow of the dashboard lights, the two men exchanged knowing smiles, like covert agents preparing for a mission of utmost importance.

"How long's it been?" Marty inquired, nodding at the tachometer, which read forty-five hundred RPMs. The roar of the engine was still drowned out by the party noise from inside the club.

To ensure success, earlier in the day, when Gil gassed up the truck, he'd added several ounces of finely-crushed charcoal to the tank. When this ignited in the engine it was going to generate a tremendous amount of carbon monoxide. And to mask the aroma of engine combustion, he had stuffed several sponge-filters commonly used for aquariums, into the end of the hose. Almost pure, unscented carbon monoxide was being pumped directly into the party.

Gil glanced at his watch, calculating the time that had passed since he rigged the air-conditioning unit. "Forty-five minutes," he replied in hushed tones, adjusting his gloves to fit his hands snugly. The satchel slung over his shoulder held all the tools and essentials they'd require once inside.

Marty slipped out of the truck, closing the door with meticulous care to avoid detection. Gil watched from the driver's seat as Marty transformed into a shadowy figure, making his way down the alley.

Donning his own balaclava and adjusting it firmly, Gil gazed at the scene through the rear-view mirror. When Marty reached the corner of the building, Gil revved the engine one last time, held it for thirty seconds, then turned off the ignition and slipped out of the truck, closing the door quietly, behind him.

Marty, now crouch-walking towards the far end of the parking lot, gripped his gun, poised for action. Gil followed, staying in the shadows. "No one is a one-man operation on a job like this," Gil reflected as he positioned himself by the air-conditioning unit. He observed the guard in front of the building and noted something peculiar about the one in the parking lot but dismissed it.

Marty looked back at Gil and offered a silent salute with his gun hand. Gil responded with a nod, a gesture of unwavering support. Marty, gun in hand, scaled a low railing separating the parking lot from the alley. He maneuvered among the parked vehicles, approaching the parking guard who seemed distracted, leaning against a truck, seemingly lost in thought.

Marty, moving stealthily, reached the opposite side of the truck from the guard. He glanced at the other guard stationed at the front door to ensure he remained preoccupied. Then, he raised his gun, taking careful aim at the back of the guard's head. A subdued pop echoed through the parking lot. Gil noted that it might have been mistaken for a cough or belch under different circumstances. The guard at the front entrance remained oblivious to the sound.

The parking guard did not immediately collapse. His head jerked forward upon impact, but something kept him upright. As Marty stood there, the young woman, who had returned to the scene, rose in front of the guard. She had been giving the guard a blowjob. At least the man had died with a smile on his face. Marty's bullet had interrupted their liaison, and her face was now adorned with a fine mist of blood from the exit wound in the front of the guard's head. Trembling, she touched her bloodied face, her hands, and her mouth. She was about to scream when Marty, his face a mask of shock and regret, shot a bullet into her left eye, ending her life with another muffled pop. She crumpled like a string cut loose, the guard's lifeless body toppling over her.

Marty stood there, gun extended, frozen in shock at the unintended consequences of his actions. Why had the girl returned? It was only supposed to be the guard who paid the price, not an innocent bystander.

The guard from the front door turned his attention toward where his partner was supposed to be. His view obstructed by a large Ford F-150, he failed to spot Marty. He called out, "Hey, Tony."

Guess the dead guy's name was Tony, Gil thought wryly, watching the front-door guard as he moved toward the far end of the parking lot to check on his comrade.

When the music abruptly ceased, the silence was almost deafening, ringing in Gil's ears. It seemed that the DJ, or whoever was responsible for the music, had finally fallen victim to the carbon monoxide. Outside the restaurant, the air stood still, as if time itself had paused. The guard redirected his focus to the front door. Marty stepped out from behind the F-150, his Glock at the ready. Gil emerged from the shadows of the building, vigilant and prepared. The guard saw Gil and called out, "Hey." His back was to the parking lot.

Marty swiftly dispatched him with a shot to the back of the head, and the guard crumpled to the sidewalk. Gil sprang into action, dragging the fallen guard into the parking lot and concealing his body behind a couple of Harley-Davidsons. Marty did the same with the parking guard and the young woman, placing her beside the guard's lifeless form. Then, he hurried back to the front door, where everything now depended on the carbon monoxide having taken effect.

Gil held the door open as Marty entered, his weapon leading the way. The front door gave way to an anteroom, serving as a coat room, and led to another set of glass doors. No one was present in the coat room, and the hangers hung vacant. Marty approached the glass doors, and Gil quietly closed the front door, keeping watch for any latecomers.

Marty reached the glass doors, finding two bodies propped against them from the inside. Flashing lights danced across the ceiling, and a mirror ball scattered laser beams throughout the room, as if these bikers were enjoying a night at a disco rather than a gang's headquarters. "Come help me with these doors," Marty whispered, and together, they pushed against the dead weight, gaining entry to the next room.

The party room was sweltering, with bodies scattered haphazardly, a chaotic tableau that someone would need to clean up. On Marty's left, a body emitted a groan, prompting him to put a bullet through its head without even a glance.

Gil, aware of the perilous carbon monoxide levels, tapped Marty on the shoulder and pointed to the basement exit. Marty nodded, and they headed in that direction. The basement door was locked, but instead of reaching for his toolkit, Marty promptly shot out the lock with his gun.

Amused, Gil couldn't help but jest, "Gonna start calling you 'The Glock-smith'."

Marty, all business and determination, pushed open the door to the basement. "You wait here for a minute, make sure no one up here comes to, or no one comes in the front door," he instructed. Gil nodded, keeping his eyes on the exterior, the weight of the operation resting on the invisible but potent presence of carbon monoxide.

Gil silently traversed the room, where lifeless bodies lay in disarray. Some rested atop tables, as if they'd fallen asleep in the middle of the party. The DJ lay sprawled over his equipment, the air conditioning still pumping air into the room. Gil was relieved he had turned off the engine, as the air was thick with the mingled scents of sweat, beer, and an oily metallic odor that could be attributed to his truck's need for a tune-up. So much for aquarium filters.

Amid the heap of bodies on the dance floor, Gil noticed a beautiful blonde woman, clad in a leather halter top and Daisy Dukes – cut-off jean shorts. Her life had been extinguished, but her neck was still warm from the exertion of dancing only minutes ago. Gil pulled one side of her halter down, out of curiosity. That was one beautiful dead breast.

The frenetic scream that tore through the basement door jolted Gil, nearly sending him tumbling onto the lifeless woman at his feet. In three swift strides, he reached the basement door, where Marty's frantic shouts urged him to halt the intruder. A half-naked, shrieking woman charged up the stairs, and Gil, overcoming his initial shock, delivered a well-aimed punch to her face. She staggered backward but regained her balance, revealing she was no demure lady. She appeared capable of taking a punch and dishing out a few in return.

Clad in distressed jeans adorned with black leather strips, Dayton boots, and covered in tattoos, she lacked a top, and her unrestrained breasts wobbled with the impact of Gil's blow, jiggling as she fought to maintain her footing by clutching the railing. Her physique was a complex blend of strength and indulgence; her biceps were formidable, but her waistline hung over her jeans, evidence of her penchant for debauchery. The tattoos did little to enhance her appeal.

She launched herself at Gil, like a mad dog. She was a flailing mass of color and tits and fists. Every punch, kick, and spit she unleashed found its mark on Gil's vulnerable body. His face absorbed the initial blows, followed by a kick to the stomach and a shoulder slam to the chest as she propelled herself toward the front doors. Yanking on the doorknob, she struggled to open it, while the bodies blocking the exit impeded her escape. These momentary obstacles allowed Marty to ascend the basement stairs and, with his Glock leveled, blow a hole in the back of her head. The exit wound sprayed the glass doors, the shimmering mirror-ball casting dancing laser lights on the blood, amplifying its vividness.

Gil was knocked flat on his back, landing atop two portly male bikers. In his attempt to rise, he became ensnared in their wallet chains. Marty, still chuckling, gazed at the disheveled Gil, whose nose bled from the encounter with the half-naked woman. Marty couldn't respond amid his laughter, and Gil wiped the blood from his face with his hands.

He offered Gil a wad of paper towels to clean himself, Marty's laughter continued. "Oh man, you should see what happened downstairs. We're lucky she didn't get out. I think she might be a cop, but I'm not entirely sure. You be the judge when you check it out."

Gil was incredulous. "A cop? You killed a cop?"

Marty replied, "Well, she might be a cop, but if she is, she's dirty. We probably did her a favor, kiddo." Marty signaled for Gil to follow him downstairs, but just as Gil began to descend, Marty placed a hand on his chest, his gaze momentarily captivated by the dead woman's exposed breast. "What the hell, Gil? What did you do?"

Gil retorted, "Nothing. She's dead. I looked. Besides, she's still warm."

Marty, diverting his gaze from the woman's breast, scrutinized Gil. "I can tolerate a lot of things, but messing with a dead woman, Gil, that's bad. You need help."

Gil remained silent, his own thoughts echoing Marty's concerns. Yet, he wasn't ashamed of his actions, refusing to apologize for doing as he pleased in a world that did as it wished to him. The rules no longer applied to Gil Tyrannus. He pushed past Marty, declaring, "I didn't do anything. I looked. That's it. Do whatever you want. Don't let me stop you."

Behind him, Marty shook his head and, reaching down, covered the dead woman's exposed breast with her jacket. As he joined Gil downstairs, he spoke loudly, "We'll have to torch this place when we're finished. I can't trust you didn't leave any evidence on her."

Gil accepted the insults but replied, "We were going to torch this place anyway. There are two gas cans in the truck, so screw you." It marked the first time Gil had used such an expression on Marty. "Fucking Glocksmith," he said derisively. Together, they descended into the basement.

In the basement, Gil inquired, "So what makes you think that screamer was a cop?" His voice still carried a trace of anger from Marty's stinging words.

Marty chuckled, "Well it was funny, kiddo. I came downstairs. I heard voices. Well, moaning or groaning, anyway. I pushed the door open a bit. The fighter upstairs was face deep between the knees of the one on the bed. I pushed the barrel into the space in the door and, pfft, got her right in the temple. The one eating didn't even notice it. She just kept going."

Marty was very energetic telling this part, he was pacing and gesticulating. "I didn't have a good second shot since the chick's thigh was between me and her head. I stepped into the room and I guess that's when she lifted her head and saw me and then also saw her friend was bleeding out the side of her head. She jumped up, caught me off guard, she dodged and zig zagged around me and headed up the stairs."

Marty was laughing at the imagery he was creating. Gil was disgusted, he wanted to end this charade, so he asked, "And how is she a cop?"

Marty pointed at the pile of clothes on the floor at the foot of the bed. A cop's uniform lay in a heap beside a pair of highly-polished black boots. At the head of the bed, on the floor, was a pile of biker-trash accoutrements, Dayton's, leather vest, Harley t-shirt and jeans. It was easy to see where the starting line was for each of the participants. Gil picked up the Cop blouse and saw a cop nametag pinned above the pocket and a notebook and pen inside. He tossed the shirt back onto the pile.

Gil was trying to bring his temper back under control. He looked at the woman's head, and said, "Good shot Marty." Then without waiting for a reply, "Let's get what we came for and get the fuck out of here." Gil led the way to the back of the basement to the room at the end of the hall.

Marty smirked, likely reminiscing about Gil's confrontation with the topless woman. He led Gil to a closed door at the end of a short hallway, beyond which lay a well-lit room with a table and chairs. Gil assumed this was their ultimate destination and followed Marty.

This dimly lit room resembled a sordid laboratory. Shelves held empty beakers and vials, while the table itself displayed scales and heaps of raw, indistinguishable substances, possibly cocaine or heroin. Across from the shelves, a table was covered with rectangular cubes wrapped in duct tape, the very objects they had come for. Gil swung his satchel around to access it and retrieved two black nylon duffle bags, tossing one to Marty. Together, they started filling the bags.

Gil's eyes scoured the room, and he asked, "Did you find any cash?"

Marty responded, "I didn't check. We had an agreement for the drugs. Still, we could look, but we gotta hurry."

Gil pondered the idea of leaving any potential cash behind. "It would be a shame to torch the place with money lying around."

Marty shook his head, insisting, "No time, kiddo. Grab your sack and let's get out of here." He had completed packing the cubes, while Gil still clutched two in his hands, lost in thought.

Determined to make his point, Gil said, "I'm not leaving cash down here. If there's all these drugs, there has to be a pile of cash, too. One goes with the other."

Marty would not be dissuaded. "Look, kiddo. We were sent here for the drugs. Boss said nothing about any cash. And you don't know, if you do something not to his liking, he can make your life a living hell." His voice trailed off and he shrugged, "I'll leave it to your imagination."

Gil scanned the room again. There wasn't anything that looked like it could conceal an amount that would justify pissing of their employer. "God damn it, Marty." Gil fondled the two bricks, idly turning them in his hands.

"Hey," Marty nudged Gil, "Pick it up, kiddo. Let's go." Gil snapped out of his reverie, tossing the last two bricks into his bag.

The two men quickly exited the clubhouse, carrying the two duffle bags, each containing twenty bricks. Gil attempted to calculate the haul and shared his excitement. "That's like, two hundred and eighty thousand dollars. We're getting about seventy? Is that right?"

Marty corrected him, "We're getting ten bricks, and they're worth ten or twelve grand each, but we have to find our own buyers."

Gil was furious, fearing their lack of contacts. "We don't know anyone to sell this stuff to. We probably just killed the only people in the area who could handle ten bricks of this shit."

Marty tried to explain, "Stan says the boss wanted it done this way. Everything with the client, it's always a test."

Gil suggested an alternative, "What if we give the client the whole lot and offer a discount? He can find a buyer. Why not do that? Fifty cents on the dollar, or even ten cents. Marty, why tell me this now? When we're done?" He discarded his balaclava into the truck and cut the duct tape securing the fire hose to the truck's exhaust pipe.

Marty crawled into the back of the truck and passed out two five-gallon, fire-engine-red gas cans. Gil carried them down the dark alley. Marty followed him. At the railing, Marty jumped over first, and took the gas cans from Gil. Marty carried the cans to the front of the building, stopped and looked both ways along the roadway, then proceeded around the corner and out of sight.

Gil went to the air conditioning unit and stripped the duct tape off the air intake. He dragged the fire hose back toward the truck. He rolled it loosely into a ball and tossed it into a bush beside the truck. Then he ran back down the alley, jumped the railing and made his way to join Marty inside.

One of the gas cans was just inside the second set of glass doors. Marty was nowhere to be seen, but Gil assumed he was down in the basement. Gil unscrewed the lid on the can and started spilling gas all around him, on the bodies of the dead bikers and their ladies, on the Deejay's turntable and speaker system. He'd spilled most of the gas around. It pooled in some spots, but mostly it soaked into the clothes and carpeting in the room. Gil tossed the empty can into the cloak roam between the double glass doors and the main entrance and stepped outside.

He watched Marty spilling the last of his gas back and forth across the stairs as he climbed backwards up them. He tossed his empty can back down into the basement. When Marty approached the double doors, he sparked a Zippo lighter that he drew from his pants pocket. A bright orange flame illuminated his face in the darkness of the vestibule. Marty stepped through and tossed the lighter behind him. The dance floor erupted in a roaring ball of flame. The heat blasted Gil in the face.

A bit of flame licked out between the double glass doors and touched Marty on the back of his head, and he squealed like a little girl. The double doors were sucked closed by the backdraft. Then the glass blackened on the fire side of the doors, obliterating their view.

Marty said, "Time to go." And they did.

Back at the truck, Gil sat in the driver's seat, he said to Marty, "This conversation is not over."

"Which conversation is that? The one where you quit with nothing to show, or the one where we find a way to sell our share?" Marty's demeanour was stern.

They continued their journey in silence, forced to halt at a red light just a block from the clubhouse. Gil noticed in the passenger-side rear view mirror, a column of smoke rising from the clubhouse's direction, gradually intensifying with sparks and heat shimmers. Soon, it transformed into a towering inferno of flames, and the wailing sirens of first responders reached their ears as the light turned green.

The thought of splitting over a hundred thousand dollars with Marty, regardless of how it was attained, crept into Gil's consciousness. Most of the jobs Stan passed them paid anywhere from a couple of hundred dollars to maybe a couple of thousand. The work was steady. It was mostly easy. And they rarely needed to kill anyone. Tonight, made up for all that, in spades. You had to crack a few eggs, was the sentiment, to make an omelet.

"Alright, shit for brains" Gil said to the back of Marty's head as the older man stared out the passenger side window. "Who and how? That's what I want to know."

Marty took his time turning his head to look at Gil. "I'll let that remark pass. This time," he stressed. "Don't forget which one of us carries a fucking gun." He wasn't smiling when he said it. Gil stopped for a red light, and turned to stare at Marty. They held like that for about twenty seconds, then both men broke and started laughing. "I fucking had you. I fucking had you, kiddo."

In the back of the limousine Gil reflected on that ancient conversation. Marty describing a contact in another part of the country that would entail a road trip of epic proportions. Gil declined to accompany his old friend.

Some weeks later, upon his return, Marty met Gil at the Sunrise and handed him his share, five bundles of hundred-dollar bills. Stan demanded his cut, but Marty reminded him he'd already received compensation from the client. Gil was grateful for Marty coming to his rescue, once again.

Later, when they were alone, Marty confided to Gil that he'd kept one of the bricks for personal use. That was at least two pounds of pure uncut heroin. Gil expressed concern for his friend. Marty was incensed. Insults were exchanged. They parted, never to work together again.

Reclining in the back of the limo, Gil lamented not having made amends back when it would have mattered. His pride always got in the way when he thought about finding Marty and making up. Even now, in the back of the limousine, after using Marty to safeguard that damn key, he thought, fuck that junkie. No small wonder Pride topped the list of deadly sins. Even when he should be grateful to the older man, he had ill feelings toward him.

Gil mulled over their conversation, his share of the proceeds, and their past disagreements. Their relationship had deteriorated after Marty kept a brick of the biker's heroin for his personal use, leading to a bitter parting. In the limousine's back seat, Gil couldn't help but recall his resentment toward Marty for that act of betrayal, viewing all junkies with disdain.

Seeing the state Marty was in, today, was justification enough that Gil was right all along. That brick was the tip of the iceberg that ruined their friendship and working relationship. To him, everyone else was weaker and inferior, granting him the license to act as he pleased, right or wrong. Gil was a criminal involved in theft, rape, and murder, but he saw himself as above junkies, whom he regarded as the worst of the dregs of society.

## FENRIZ ABADDON

Gil Tyrannus reclined in the opulent limousine, deep in thought. He found himself caught in an identity crisis. A tapestry of crimes and misdeeds defined him. He was more and he was also less. The past lingered like an uninvited guest, and Gil tired of these memories, punctuated only by sips of bottled water. Thirty minutes had passed since they'd left the Sunrise. His gaze wandered out to the passing suburban homes.

They travelled through a residential neighborhood, devoid of the typical urban clutter, without low-rises or duplexes. These single-family homes were set on wide, secluded lots, reminiscent of the places he once targeted for his break-and-enters. His mind shifted into a familiar mode, one honed by years of reconnaissance and criminal intent. He noted CCTV cameras, pondered escape routes, and cataloged potential vulnerabilities for future reference.

The limousine slowed, signaling their imminent entry into a gated driveway. Luxury vehicles approached from the opposite direction: Ferraris, BMWs, and high-end SUVs. Gil's mind instinctively shifted into his casing-the-joint mentality. He scrutinized the surroundings, mentally mapping the security measures.

The limo crossed the street and passed through the gate, revealing a scene that defied his expectations. Rather than a multi-level mansion with an array of windows, they found themselves amidst a sprawling driveway and overgrown hedges. The gate closed behind them, sealing them off from the outside world.

The thick hedge loomed like a foreboding tunnel, swallowing them in darkness. The car's headlights pierced the gloom, brushing against encroaching branches. The cold air conditioning in the car seemed to

intensify, but Gil hesitated to request warmth, unwilling
to show vulnerability. He knew the chill was not just
from the frigid air but from the adrenaline coursing
through his veins.

The only source of light was the dashboard, casting a
shadowy silhouette of the driver who remained watchful
through the rear-view mirror. As the limo inched
forward, Gil struggled to discern the vehicle's speed and
the details outside. Shadows melded into one another,
and he pressed his face against the window, straining to
identify any shapes within the darkness.

Suddenly, a face emerged from the shadows, screaming
and pounding the glass with white-knuckled fists. Gil let
out a startled scream, recoiling as the car exited the
hedgerow into the late afternoon light. It had been over
two decades, but he recognized the face of the female
guard Marty had shot during their first heist.

Breathing heavily, he turned toward the driver and
shouted, "What the hell was that?"

The driver, unperturbed, asked, "What the hell was what,
sir?" His gaze remained steady in the rear-view mirror as
the car came to a stop.

Gil leaped out of the limo and retreated a few paces,
attempting to scan the shadows. He couldn't see anything
or anyone in the depths of the hedge-lined driveway. He
hesitated to step further into the darkness. The wind
whispered, "Run."

Gil stood his ground, uneasy but determined. "Spooky," he mumbled under his breath.

The driver, ever unflappable, urged him, "Best not to keep the boss waiting. He's not the waiting kind of guy."

Reluctantly, Gil returned to the limo. He marveled at the colossal home before him. "Is this a hotel? This place is enormous. Where in the hell are we?"

The driver disclosed, "We're quite far south in the city, near the water, though it's not visible from here. It's on the other side of the house."

Gil took in the vastness of the building, comparing it to a castle rather than a residence. Fueled by curiosity and the surreal nature of the location, he finally inquired about the mysterious client.

"Okay, look. I've never asked about the client, but this place is beyond belief. I need to know. Who is this guy?" He grabbed the driver's arm, seeking answers.

The driver removed Gil's hand with a detached air. "I'm not at liberty to say. You'll find out soon enough, if he decides to tell you."

Resigned to the driver's discretion, Gil shifted his approach. "Alright. What's your name?"

The driver led him to the mansion's entrance and responded, "I don't have one."

Upon entering the mansion, the darkness within felt even more impenetrable than the shadows outside. Gil hesitated, feeling an unexpected chill that couldn't be attributed to the car's air conditioning. The door slammed shut, enveloping him in absolute darkness.

"Where'd you go?" Gil called out, hearing shuffling and the sound of labored breathing. The sensation of being watched bore down upon him.

A click resounded through the dimly lit corridor, and the lights in the opulent foyer suddenly blazed to life, casting Gil and the driver in stark relief. Gil fixed a piercing gaze on the driver, his voice laced with suspicion. "Are you fucking with me?" he demanded.

A wry, enigmatic smile crept across the driver's face, a hint of amusement in his eyes. "Just a little," he confessed before striding down a dimly lit hallway. With a curt motion, he beckoned Gil to follow. "This way."

As Gil took a moment to survey his surroundings, the grandeur of the mansion washed over him. A sweeping, semi-circular staircase led to an ornate second-floor landing, adorned with a meticulously carved wooden railing that emphasized the curve of the staircase. There was no ceiling to speak of, only an expansive chandelier suspended high above the foyer. The walls were cloaked in luxurious velvet, embossed with intricate scenes of exotic animals. The floor beneath him was a dazzling mosaic, meticulously crafted to depict the night sky, with black and white marble artistry forming constellations

and galaxies that stretched across the entire entryway.
Curious cubby holes housed small statues of nude men
and women, frozen in various provocative poses.

Impatience dripped from the driver's voice as he barked
at Gil, "Hey, Tyrannus. This way, I said."

Gil raised an eyebrow, sarcasm oozing from his tone. "I
thought I was Mister Tyrannus to you. Where are we
headed, anyway?"

"Library," came the curt reply from the terse driver. He
came to a halt in front of another ornate door,
considerably smaller than the main entryway doors.
"You can wait in here. The Master will be with you
shortly."

Gil's incredulity was palpable. "Did you just say
'Master'? Who in the hell calls anyone 'Master' in this
day and age?"

The driver appeared visibly embarrassed, casting a
furtive glance, and then ushered Gil into the lavishly
appointed room. He spun on his heel, firmly closing the
heavy door behind him. Gil glanced around the room, his
gaze absorbing the decadence that surrounded him.

The library was indeed a colossal chamber, with soaring
ceilings that seemed to scrape the heavens. Towering
bookshelves lined three walls, their contents an eclectic
blend of the arcane and the mysterious. Four ladders on
wheels stretched toward the lofty shelves, their

mechanisms promising access to untold knowledge. Two high-backed, over-stuffed chairs sat in silent conversation before a gigantic fireplace, a small table between them, adorned with a decanter and two crystal glasses.

Intriguing objects occupied each corner of the room, encased in glass bell jars. Curiosity drew Gil to the closest one, positioned along the same wall as the entrance. A suspended light from the ceiling cast a warm glow on the contents – a small, hand-crafted wooden box adorned with dozens of crosses etched into its sides. The Gothic script across the top bore the name "Arriens." The wood appeared well-worn, leaving no clues about its purpose or value.

Gil ventured to the next artifact, his eyes briefly scanning the spines of the ancient books. Some were weathered and worn, written in languages foreign to him. His eyes caught the occasional word, like "Inquisitor" or "Daemon." The second bell jar cradled three candles, handmade and aged. Once white, time had tinged them yellow, and Gil squinted to examine an oddity in the wax. Could that be a fingernail? A human fingernail? It seemed improbable, yet Gil's curiosity persisted.

As he neared the third bell jar, passing by the recently used fireplace with its pungent scent of burnt wood, Gil wondered if he was the victim of an elaborate prank. He peered inside, only to find something one might discover at a novelty shop in town – a human skull resting on a bed of black velvet. But it was no ordinary skull. Two small, vestigial horns protruded on either side of its forehead. Gil squinted, attempting to discern a seam between the horns and the skull itself, but the glass distorted his view. His skepticism mounted. Could this be anything other than a grotesque joke? And where the hell was this 'Master'?

Before Gil could investigate the last bell jar, which appeared to house a scroll of some kind, the library door creaked open. A diminutive figure entered. The driver held the door open. A moment of silence hung between them, broken by the unexpected words that escaped the small man's lips. "I thought you'd be taller," he said, offering a disarming smile as he extended his hand. "I am Fenriz Abaddon, Mister Tyrannus. May I call you Gil? Please call me Fen. My closest associates all do." The driver closed the door and took up a position outside the library.

Gil recoiled, surprised by the man's stature. Abaddon was not only half Gil's height but possessed a presence that defied his physical form – slender, with close-cropped white hair that defied his apparent age. Their handshake revealed a surprising strength, undermining any notions of underestimating Abaddon. "I'm sorry for keeping you waiting," Abaddon continued. "I see you've been exploring. What do you think of the library?"

Gil's gaze traveled upward, taking in the cavernous expanse that seemed to defy the laws of architectural space. "This place is huge," he mused. "I think my whole apartment is smaller than this room. And that fireplace could roast a full-grown pig."

Abaddon's response was nonchalant, though chilling. "Yes, it can, and it has, many times."

Gil gestured toward the peculiar contents of the bell jars. "Is this some sort of joke?"

Abaddon's response only deepened the mystery. "Oh, you don't like my little collection?" Abaddon caressed the bell jar preserving the skull. "This unfortunate individual grew subcutaneous horns, and he was beaten and beheaded by a mob in India. I acquired the head a few years ago. It's one of my favorite curiosities."

Gil's incredulity extended to the candles – the suspicion evident in his wrinkled nose. "Human tallow? Made from human fat?"

"That's correct. They are very important pieces of my collection. I collect. It's what I do Mister Tyrannus," Abaddon confirmed.

Gil shifted his discomfort and requested, "Yeah, definitely call me Gil. The 'Mister' part is making me uncomfortable."

Leaning closer to the candles, Abaddon offered another disconcerting revelation. "If you look closely, Gil, you might spot some hairs in the wax. The candle-makers weren't known for their perfectionism."

Curiosity led Gil to the first bell jar he had examined, only for Abaddon to issue a warning. "I wouldn't get too close to that one, Gil, just to be safe. It contains the ashes and some bone fragments from a witch burning."

"Salem?" Gil inquired, seeking to make sense of the unsettling artifacts.

Abaddon corrected him with a touch of historical insight. "No, not at all. This is from one of the last witch burnings, in Holland during the Sixteenth century. It was an exciting time to be a witch in Europe for about two hundred years, and witchcraft remained novel in the New World as late as 1690. Besides, the witches in Salem were hanged, not burned. If you're interested, I have one of the ropes used for that purpose, in another room."

Concern etched Gil's features as he contemplated the possible dangers of the witch's ashes. "Are the ashes radioactive or something? Why should I avoid getting close?"

Abaddon offered a cryptic warning, his tone betraying nothing. "It's likely just an old wives' tale, but some say she can possess you if you get too close. I'm not entirely convinced she's really dead."

Puzzled but inexplicably compelled to remain, Gil pressed on. "I didn't get to the last bell jar. What's inside that one?" he inquired, pointing toward the remaining curiosity.

Abaddon's eyes sparkled with intrigue. "That, Gil, holds something of even greater value and significance than the witch's ashes. It's a piece of the Dead Sea Scrolls that I had translated and carbon-dated. I believe it to be authentic in every respect. This fragment details the temptation of Christ in the desert, but in this version, the Devil plays the role of the hero." He chuckled at that.

Gil couldn't suppress his curiosity, and he looked up at his peculiar host. "May I ask you some personal questions? Forgive me if I seem impertinent."

Abaddon, ever patient, crossed his arms and tilted his head with anticipation. "Please, go ahead, but tread carefully. My feelings are easily hurt." His disarming smile remained in place.

Gil glanced skyward, selecting his words with care, and leaned against one of the high-backed chairs. "Do you own this place, the mansion, and the property? I must admit, I've never seen this part of town, and I've explored most corners of the city."

Abaddon confirmed his ownership with nonchalance. "Yes, I do own this house. I had it painstakingly transported, stone by stone, from Northern England."

Undeterred, Gil pressed further, "Alright, so you're wealthy, and you certainly seem intelligent. But I'm confused. You appear to be easily fooled – a fake skull, mysterious ashes, old candles, ancient parchment. What's the story here? You're starting to look like the most elaborate mark I've ever encountered. Forgive me if that offends you, but I'm baffled."

Abaddon's response was enigmatic as ever. "What if I told you that all these curiosities are genuine, and all were acquired at great sacrifice." He leaned forward, "Would proof convince you? Would you believe me then?"

Gil remained cautiously skeptical. "It depends on the proof, I suppose."

Abaddon gestured for them to take a seat, their conversation veering into a strange area that transcended reality. As they shared a rare Armagnac, Abaddon delved into Gil's past, revealing his meticulous knowledge and cunning insight.

Fen sat back in his chair, crossed his knee, and said, "Gil, how long have you worked for me?"

Gil felt ambushed. He smiled, and said, "I don't work for you. I work for myself. Always have. I was an apprentice for three years, then had my own company until the market went for a shit. And then I worked for, I mean with, Marty for about twenty years. Other than that, I've never worked for anyone but myself."

It was Fen's turn to smile, and he did so broadly. He said, "I know all about your history, Gil. There is little about you that I do not know. I knew your Master-locksmith and compensated him very well to pay close attention to your education. I watched with joy as you succeeded in your chosen field, and I was saddened when, as you say, it all went for a shit." Fen took another sip of his Armagnac. "I watched you struggle with failure," he raised a hand when Gil objected. "Not your fault, I'm aware, but what happened next was entirely your choice. Do you recall what happened next?"

"You mean when I met Marty?" Gil's brow furrowed. Where was this little man taking him? His knowledge of Gil's life was unsettling.

"Precisely. He introduced you at the Sunrise Tavern. You watched Stan nearly kill a man. You helped Marty move the victim, and when left alone with a choice, you sacrificed a dying man's life to a garbage dumpster. That was quite the choice you made. Do you think it was the right one?" Fen tented his fingers and leaned forward in his seat, anticipating Gil's response.

"I do." Said Gil. Fen waited in silence for him to continue. Gil hated feeling manipulated, but when the other man sat there in silence, waiting, Gil spoke, "Up until I met Marty, I'd been putting everyone else ahead of me. Parents, employees, dying men. Fuck that, I thought, fuck that. It's time to put me first, and so I did. To hell with that guy. He was going to be dead in a couple of minutes anyway. I remember I looked into the dumpster to see if he'd at least be comfortable. Then I tossed him in. So what? No harm. Who cares?" Gil sat back, drained from the exertion of remembering the events of that day and his so-called fall from grace, that defining moment when he'd let go of caring about anyone, and sought only to please himself going forward.

Fen fell backwards into the comfortable chair and let out a laugh. "That's fantastic. 'Who cares?' I love it." Fen sipped his Armagnac and stared at Gil, as if he was examining a bug under a microscope. Then he said, "I assume that the driver who brought you here today, was unfamiliar to you? There was no hint of recognition?" Gil shook his head in the negative and he frowned. Fen continued, "That's hilarious. 'Who cares?'"

Fen's voice cut through the tension in the room and loudly proclaimed to be heard through the library door. "Dante," he shouted, emphasizing the name with a certain weight. The driver, Dante, entered the room. "Do you recognize this man?"

Dante, observed Gil with an unreadable gaze. "I drove him here, is that what you mean?" His reply was layered with a tinge of ambiguity.

Fen leaned back, swirling the Armagnac in his glass, the moment stretching like the suspenseful pause before a critical revelation. "No," he declared, "Had you seen him prior to today? Do you recognize him from a previous encounter?"

Dante's squinted eyes conveyed more questions than answers. "No. Should I?" he responded, still assessing Gil.

Fen relished the situation. "He's the reason you're here, with me," he disclosed, his words laden with intrigue.

Dante nodded, showing loyalty. "Well then, I should thank you, Mister Tyrannus. Master Abaddon has been very good to me these past twenty years," he acknowledged. The conversation hung in the air, shrouded in secrecy.

Fen's cryptic demeanor continued, emphasizing his control over the situation. "Is that other matter taken care of?" he inquired.

Dante affirmed, "Yes, sir. He's in the foyer awaiting further instructions."

"Excellent," Fen replied, dismissing Dante. The driver exited the library, leaving Fen and Gil alone, once more. Fen filled their drinks and offered the glass to Gil, maintaining the air of intrigue and power.

Gil swallowed his Armagnac in one defiant gulp. "What was that supposed to prove? Was he the guy from the dumpster?" he asked, his skepticism evident.

Fen nodded knowingly. "Small world," he mused, the words dripping with sarcasm. He scrutinized Gil, preparing for a revelation. "Gil Tyrannus," he began, leaning forward with a purpose, "Despite your objections, you have always worked for me."

Gil's eyes flared with a mixture of anger and disbelief, but Fen silenced him. "Listen to me," he continued. "It is

I who directed Marty to recruit you and Stan to employ you. Every job you were tasked with was for me. You were never told about the clients for your various jobs, but it was never anyone else, but me. Me! For all intents and purposes, I own you. We'll let that sink in for a moment, shall we?"

Gil's seething hatred swirled like a tempest within him. He broke eye contact with Fen, surveying the room that emitted a facade of opulence but lacked true wealth, much like Fen himself. Gil's focus shifted back, and he decided to hear the little man out, for now.

"What did you bring me here for?" Gil asked, his earlier contempt still palpable. "I didn't want to meet you at all, but now that I have, I have to admit, you are kind of a disappointment."

Fen chuckled softly. "Believe me, you're not the first person to be underwhelmed by me. You won't be the last," he said, embodying his baffling charm.

Fen reached for an old, worn book, emphasizing his eccentricity. "What I have here is a treasure map, of sorts," he disclosed.

Gil's derisive laughter filled the room. "Treasure map! Are you fucking kidding me? You're either stupid or you're trying to run a scam?" he scoffed; disbelief painted across his face.

With a bold move, Gil turned to leave. He threw open the door, stepped out into the hallway and stormed into the foyer. He came to an abrupt halt when he saw Marty seated in a chair next to the front door. Dante descended the staircase at a run to his Master's defense.

Marty jumped up, his face bright and smiling. "Hey kiddo. I see you've met Mister Abaddon." The look on his face was meant to calm Gil.

Incredulous, Gil shouted in disbelief, "What the hell are you doing here?"

Gil was cognizant of the fact that Marty probably still had the key in his possession. The abrupt encounter with Marty in the foyer interrupted his exit. As he met Marty's eyes, unspoken signals regarding the hidden key were exchanged, adding another layer of intrigue to the situation. Dante, the ever-vigilant driver, stood ready to prevent any premature departure.

Fen appeared at the library door, calm and composed, and addressed the trio. "Dante, stand down, please. Gil, I need you to come back and hear me out. If you decline this job, I won't stop you from leaving." Fen's words masked deeper motives, while Marty played his part in persuading Gil to stay.

Reluctantly, Gil agreed to stay and listen. Fen's face relaxed into a relieved smile as he guided the group back into the library, humming a mysterious tune. In the library he gestured for Dante to bring another chair and for Gil and Marty to be seated. He then signalled for Dante to stand by the door. Fen sat and poured himself another glass of Armagnac.

Gil noticed that when Marty sat down, he had to adjust himself to find a comfortable position. He was carrying his weapon in the usual place, in the small of his back, in the waistband. Apparently, Dante did not frisk him. Or he didn't care.

When they were settled, Fen held out his hand, palm up, in expectation, toward Marty. The international sign for, give me the key. Marty looked sheepishly at Gil. He reached into his shirt pocket and pulled out the small plastic box that held the obsidian key and placed it into Fen's outstretched hand. Fen said, "Thank you." He placed the key case onto the small table in between the three men.

Gil was livid. Traitor! He then held his hand out to Marty, palm up. It took a few seconds for Marty to realize what was being demanded. He chuckled, then Marty produced the two hundreds and placed them into Gil's hand. Maintaining eye contact with Marty, Gil slid the bills into his shirt pocket and returned his attention to Fen and the obsidian key.

Fen addressed Gil, "I want to tell you about the significance of this key."

Gil tapped an impatient fingertip on the small plastic box, "You know, you still haven't paid me for this thing."

Fen replied, "We'll get there. Robbing you is beneath me."

Gil sat back and rolled his eyes. He pinched the bridge of his nose. "You're giving me a headache, Fen. You really are. Okay, when I'm ready to leave there better be a stack of hundreds leaving with me."

Fen agreed. "Of course. But listen to me." Brandishing the book, he began, "This book is over four-hundred years old. It is the journal of one of the earliest explorers in this country. Were you aware that Christopher Columbus was an evil man? He beat and tortured his crew to make them obey. He beat and tortured the native population when he arrived in the New World. And all of this was condoned by the Catholic church at the time. Does that surprise you?"

Gil sneered, "Nothing about the Catholic church surprises me."

"It's all here in this journal. One of the novice monks fell in love with an indigenous woman, whom sadly he never names, and together they ran away from Columbus and her people and they lived off the land and found themselves at odds with the woman's tribe. Understandably, of course. The monk represented all the cruelty that Columbus brought to the New World.

The monk's name was Fernando Perez. He was one of two bothers who accompanied Columbus on his journeys – Juan Perez was the other. Juan eventually became confessor to Queen Isabella upon his return to Spain. Fernando's life, although, took on new meaning in the New World. He never did return to Spain. Instead, he brought Christianity to this woman's tribe. They later killed him for the courtesy, in a most cruel method. They baked him into a clay pot, while alive. Back home in Spain, Fernando was defrocked, in absentia, by his own brother."

Gil was getting bored. He said, "So, what does all that have to do with what you need me for?"

Fen smiled. He said, "One of the reasons Fernando was killed, according to this journal, was that he had convinced the woman's tribe to gather all their treasure and give it to him for safekeeping. He was convinced that Queen Isabella was going to use this bounty to finance a war against Portugal.

The natives were an artistic people. They smelted almost pure gold and they knew how to polish gemstones. According to Fernando's journal, the people accumulated nearly two tons of gold and gems and gave it all to him, for safekeeping. In today's market, that is valued at just over eighty million dollars. Fernando, confronted with this mass of gold and wealth beyond his imaginings, decided that God had gifted this treasure to him, and him alone."

Suddenly animated and inspired, Fen continued his tale. He was on the edge of his seat when he held the book out and whispered reverentially, "And do you want to know what this young idiot did? He had two tons of gold. Do you have any idea what he did?"

"Of course not. Jesus! What did he do?" Gil exchanged looks with Marty. Eyes were rolling.

Fen continued, "Fernando built a wagon." Gil's jaw dropped. "Yes, a wagon. He loaded all the gold and gems into it and transported it as far away from the natives and Columbus as he could. And, unbelievably, he got it all the way across the continent. In his journal he describes his trek from the Atlantic Ocean to the Pacific, though he didn't know it was the Pacific when he saw it. He thought he'd walked in a three-thousand-mile circle and ended up back where he started. It only took six months to get there. He was a very strange and determined man. Even for a novice monk."

"All by himself? He dragged a wagon with two tons of gold across eight thousand miles of country, alone?"

"Oh, no. Not alone. He convinced half a dozen young tribesmen to accompany him. He abandoned his woman and left with the men. According to his notes, he had no idea how big the country was. His sole purpose was to hide the gold.

Fernando buried the treasure at the bottom of a cave. He drew a very detailed map of where it was. He killed the six braves, in their sleep and buried them with the treasure, just like any number of pirates might have done in his era. And to top it all off, he set traps to prevent thieves from making off with his treasure.

Then he did something even more mysterious. He wanted to see if he'd really walked in a circle. He walked back the way he came and less than six months later, he was reunited with the woman who was now living back with her tribe. They held a welcome home party. When he explained what he'd done and where the tribe's gold now was, they put him in a pot, and baked him into it. His journal ends with him describing how he helped them build this large pot out of clay, in his words '...with capacity of a full-grown man...'"

Fen opens the book to the last entry and shows it to Gil. Gil takes it and tries to read the handwritten words. "For fucks sake. Is that Latin?"

"Yes."

Gil considers Fen Abaddon, as if he's a lunatic. "I don't know how to break it to you. But I can't read Latin." Gil held the book out for Fen to take it back.

Fen declined. He pointed at the last line, "I assure you. That's what that line translates to."

With the book in Gil's hands, Fen flips to the next page with his index finger. A hand-drawn picture of a pot is shown, it has handles and a lid. Gil assumes that might be a drawing of the pot in which the monk was baked. "See" said Fen. And then he flipped back a few pages until he stopped at a hand-drawn map. "Compare the two drawings."

Gil flipped back and forth between the map and the pot. He did this a couple of times. He said, "They're not drawn by the same person?"

Fen, the mastermind behind this peculiar quest, nodded in agreement. "No, Gil. It appears as though two different hands brought these images to life. One, presumably a tribe member, sketched the pot. The other, maybe one of his companions, chronicled Fernando's journey. But someone took possession of this journal, and just look at its condition."

Gil carefully examined the cover and the earlier entries in the journal, then turned back to the map, his brow furrowing with concentration. "Alright, it's old, no doubt. But the mere age of a map doesn't guarantee a ton of gold."

Fen shook his head, his voice low and steady. "Gil, I've had this artifact carbon-dated. It predates Christopher Columbus's time. There are traces of blood, and I've had those analyzed. One sample is of indigenous origin, a woman, while the other is of Spanish ancestry, a man. Now, tell me, do you see anything on that map that sparks recognition?"

Gil kept a thumb on the map page, turning the book at various angles, scrutinizing the details. Fen's question lingered in the air. The map depicted mountains in the north, bodies of water, bays, inlets, landmasses, and more water. A hint of recognition struck him. "If I squint, it resembles the Vancouver coastline. The landmass would be Vancouver, the mountains — North Vancouver, the inlet is Indian Arm, and Deep Cove. Is this supposed to be Deep Cove?" Gil asked, pointing at a specific location.

Fen's excitement was nearly palpable. "Yes, Gil, that's it. Thanks to modern satellites, I've thoroughly scoured the entire Pacific Rim, and this location aligns best with the map. I believe Fernando journeyed across America and concealed his treasure somewhere nearby."

Gil thumbed through the journal again, still perplexed. "But it doesn't provide a clear spot for the treasure, just a coastline map. Where's the classic 'X' that marks the spot?"

Fen leaned closer. His voice resolute. "There are clues in the journal that point to two potential locations: Deep Cove and east Vancouver. Deep Cove has a promising cave system, and in east Vancouver, there's a filled-in ravine that currently serves as a graveyard with crypts that extend deep underground. I've secured the cave property and the deepest crypt. I've done my homework, and I'm convinced there's two tons of gold waiting to be claimed."

Gil, still skeptical, threw the journal back into Fen's lap. "So, why do you need me? Just go and claim your treasure."

Fen remained unfazed by Gil's outburst, calmly gesturing for the journal to be passed around the room. Dante, their driver, obligingly took it, and Marty placed the journal back on the bookshelf. During this, Fen sat back, closed his eyes, and took deep breaths, as if preparing for a pivotal revelation.

Then, with sudden intensity, Fen's eyes snapped open, fixing on Gil. "What I'm about to disclose will strain belief, and you may not believe it."

Gil, a mix of amusement and incredulity in his eyes, quipped, "Do you really think I've believed anything you've said so far?"

Fen pressed on, his tone grave. "The journal narrates Fernando's journey from the Atlantic to the Pacific while carrying two tons of gold. It speaks of encounters with ferocious beasts, such as wolves and buffalo, his isolation, despair, and relentless fear. He intentionally avoided other tribes, nearly starving. His journey was rife with sacrifice and trials, but he succeeded."

Fen paused for dramatic effect -- his words heavy with anticipation. "And then, at the end of his strength, near his last breath, he crested a hill and beheld the vast Pacific Ocean, knowing at last that the treasure was safe from Columbus. He discovered a cave that plunged deep into the earth."

Fen refilled their glasses, catching Gil by surprise as he downed his drink in a single gulp. Clearly, he needed a moment of liquid courage.

Gil took this moment to ask a relevant question, "So, what the fuck is the key for, then?"

"I'll get to that presently." Fen leaned back his expression inscrutable. "Gil, the real story in that journal isn't about the journey but what Fernando found inside that cave."

Gil's curiosity was piqued, and he leaned forward.

Fen whispered conspiratorially, "Fernando writes that he encountered the Devil inside that cave."

Gil couldn't help but chuckle. "Oh no! Not the Devil?" He laughed out loud and tried to make eye-contact with Marty who stared stubbornly at the floor. Dante's expression was livid with rage. Gil turned his attention back to Abaddon. "That's it! I'm not taking any more of your bullshit. You need to pay me now. I'm done. I want my money." Gil stood before Fenriz, clenching and unclenching his fists. His face flushed dark red. He was apoplectic.

When Dante took a step further into the room, Fen stayed him with a glance. To Gil, Fen invited him to resume his seat. Gil reluctantly complied.

"I take it you're an unbeliever?" Fen's lips smiled but his eyes burned holes into Gil.

"Something like that." Gil replied, his disdain was palpable.

"Prince of Darkness, Fallen Angel, Lord of the Flies? Not your thing?"

"Hardly."

Fen smiled ruefully and said, "You'd be a fan of Beaudelaire, then. They attribute him with 'the greatest trick the Devil ever pulled was convincing the world he didn't exist.' It doesn't matter what either of us believes. I know what Fernando's diary states."

Fen's next revelation hit like a thunderclap. "The Devil said that he would only allow someone utterly corrupt to access the treasure—someone devoid of empathy, compassion, or love. The treasure can only be claimed by someone ruined."

"Ruined?"

"Corrupt. Irredeemable."

"I know what ruined means." Gil's skepticism waned, and he drained his glass, then poured another. His attitude shifted from amusement to astonishment. "You're suggesting that I'm the right kind of 'ruined'?"

Fen's explanation continued, "Marty's reports on you have been thorough. Over time, you've shown a remarkable transformation. You've shed inhibitions, ignored laws and moral norms, and become progressively more ruthless. You've proven yourself to be someone with no regard for others, driven only by self-interest. You're exactly what the Devil desires: thoroughly corrupt and devoid of any moral restraint."

Staring at his oh-so-gracious host, Gil pondered the implications. He glanced at Marty, who now returned his gaze, and Dante, who was blocking the exit. Then he faced Fen with a crucial question.

"Why me? Why specifically choose me when you have capable people like Marty and even your driver? What's the reason?"

Fen leaned in and poured Gil another glass of Armagnac, taking his time. Gil suspected that Fen was stalling. Finally, Fen revealed the last piece of the puzzle.

"According to the journal, only someone with no trace of goodness inside them can lay claim to the treasure. The Devil's conditions are clear. It must be someone utterly, irredeemably corrupt, devoid of empathy, compassion, or love. You fit that description perfectly, Gil."

As the gravity of this revelation sunk in, Gil found himself at a crossroads, faced with the allure of an unimaginable fortune and the weight of his own moral degradation.

Fen's eyes glinted with a blend of excitement and caution as Gil's world shifted beneath him. It was an internal dance of shadows and secrets, a tapestry woven with threads of betrayal and a treasure trove beyond imagination.

"The key?" Gil demanded.

"There's a door. The monk took the wagon apart and constructed a door deep within the cave barricading the gold within."

The room grew heavy with the weight of Fen's revelation. The old man's gaze bore into Gil's soul as he continued to paint a chilling picture of a descent into darkness.

Marty, sat back in his seat, looked at Gil with a mix of regret and dread. It was clear he had been a willing participant in this game, but the full magnitude of Fen's plan was only now coming to light.

Gil's voice was filled with uncertainty as he muttered, "So, you want me to retrieve this treasure for you because I'm...what...vile?"

Fen leaned in, his eyes never leaving Gil's. "Yes," he said, his voice dripping with conviction. "You see, Gil, the Devil is an entity of malevolence, a being that thrives on corruption and wickedness. According to Fernando's account, only someone truly impure can approach that treasure without suffering the Devil's wrath. And, as I've come to understand, you, my dear friend, are the perfect candidate."

Gil's mind was spinning with the implications of it all. Eighty million dollars was a tantalizing prospect, but it was now shackled to a sinister quest, one that required him to embrace his darkest impulses. Could he really become the embodiment of corruption to retrieve a treasure buried by a man who met the Devil himself?

Fen, sensing the weight of Gil's internal turmoil, reached across the table and placed a hand on his. "I understand that this is a lot to take in, Gil. But think about it, consider the opportunity before you. You have a chance to make history, to challenge the very forces of evil. What's more, you can walk away with untold riches. Are you truly willing to turn your back on this?"

As Gil contemplated his next move, the room seemed to close in around him. The shadows played on the walls like specters of temptation, and the air grew colder with the magnitude of his decision that created a web from which there might be no escape. The treasure, the Devil, and his own moral descent lay before him, a tempting and dangerous path.

Marty stepped back into the conversation, his demeanor cool and calculated as he reclaimed his seat. He leaned close to Gil and spoke, his voice carrying weight. "Gil, I want you to understand something. I've always had a certain fondness for you. But you must realize, I work for Mister Abaddon. Every detail of our operations, every decision made, every move you've ever taken, I reported it all to him. He was particularly interested in you, Gil. He wanted to know your reactions to choices, challenges, and the people we encountered."

Gil felt a rush of heat to his face, his suspicions confirmed. "So, you betrayed me, Marty?"

Fen intervened, coming to Marty's aid with a measured tone. "No, Gil, you misunderstand. Marty's reports were glowing. You've proven to be precisely what I needed. Over time, you've shed your inhibitions, disregarding laws, social norms, and basic human kindness. Let's review your record: from your first encounter with Marty, you ignored a man's death and threw a living human being into a dumpster. At the blood bank job, you exhibited the potential for violence. You hardly flinched when Marty killed that woman. You've committed heinous acts on other jobs, especially those destined for destruction, erasing all DNA evidence. You've killed, stolen, and shown a complete lack of concern for anyone but yourself. You, my dear Gil, are precisely the type of person the Devil is seeking. Corrupt, and, no offense, but by any moral standard, vile."

It was impossible for Gil to dispute any of what Fen said. He looked at Marty. His old partner sat unperturbed. His voice was icy when he said, "Still a fucking rat-thing to do. And you know what happens to rats, right Marty."

Fen once again played peacemaker, "Gil, let's not resort to violence. Sacrifices must be made by all of us. I understand your anger, and it might serve you well. According to Fernando's journal, there are traps in the cave system. Fernando himself didn't emerge unscathed from his encounter with the Devil. He documented it extensively."

With eighty million dollars hanging in the balance, Gil shelved his anger for the moment. He knew he couldn't let Marty get away with this betrayal. Turning to Fen, he asked, "Tell me more."

"The cave system in Deep Cove may not be our best bet. I've had teams exploring through them. They are deep enough to be the caves described in the journal. But after much soul searching, I've decided it's best to try the graveyard in east Vancouver."

Fen continued, "We have a good idea of the cave system's location, beneath the cemetery. I've purchased the crypt above ground and some of the neighboring plots, to maintain secrecy. We've gathered all the necessary spelunking equipment and assigned Marty and Dante to accompany and assist you."

Gil's temper flared, "A junkie and a once-dead man? You're kidding, right? They'll be more trouble than they're worth."

Fen reassured him, "Don't underestimate Marty. He may look different now, but he's still capable. As for Dante, once he recovered from that beating and our rescue from the dumpster, he's been fine. Here are the maps."

With that, Fen rose from his seat and made his way to a bookshelf hidden in the corner. With a firm push, the entire bookshelf slid aside to reveal a concealed room, illuminated by a ceiling light. The interior room was adorned with pegs and shelves along three of its walls. Coils of rope dangled from some pegs, while pitons, helmets equipped with lamps, and climbing shoes scattered across shelves and the floor.

Fen gestured to Gil, instructing him to prepare himself. "Equip yourself, Gil. Take what you require. The maps are right here."

Fen picked up two cardboard tubes capped with shimmering silver, tossing them to Marty, who promptly unrolled two maps. One displayed a satellite view of the targeted area, and Gil couldn't help but notice its striking similarity to the image depicted in Fernando's journal. Everything was beginning to fall into place, though the concept of treasure remained a challenging notion to embrace.

The second map unveiled a hand-drawn rendition of the cave system, which appeared deep and perilous but still within the realm of feasibility. The entrance to this labyrinth lay in the middle of an unlikely location: a graveyard. On the spookiness scale, it scored at least a three-point-five out of ten. The entrance was concealed beneath a family crypt, ensuring that no curious bystanders would observe their descent into the cave.

As Gil stood up and ventured into the room concealed behind the bookshelves, he selected and tested several pairs of climbing shoes, settling on a pair that satisfied him. The chosen footwear found its place in a satchel, a striking indigo bag adorned with a white racing stripe. Gil contemplated the satchel's quality, silently acknowledging that it was high time he had a new one.

He added a fifty-foot coil of rope, a yellow helmet with an LED headlamp, a dozen pitons, clamps, and one of the lighter axes to his growing collection of gear.

Fen's conversation with Marty grew tiresome, diverting the old man's attention from the preparations. Gil's mind drifted to the possibilities that a forty-million-dollar share of the treasure could offer. He ruminated on the words Fen had used to describe him, as relayed by Marty. The presence of Dante in the equation was a problem, and Gil harbored deep reservations about working alongside Marty and Dante. The allure of the figure eighty-million-dollars began to outweigh the initial promise of forty, and Gil's decision became unequivocal. Perhaps one of Fen's sins was right — greed. It was time to put anger and greed into action.

Gil, satisfied with the contents of his satchel, tossed it on the floor beside Marty and Fen, interrupting their conversation with a start. Marty reacted with a slight jump, while Fen responded with a disapproving scowl. Gil moved to Marty's side, his hand reaching for the small of Marty's back, where he suspected a concealed gun resided. In one fluid motion, Gil withdrew the weapon, disengaged the safety, and chambered a round.

Dante was a mere three steps away. In the time it took for the driver to react and take two steps, Gil's arm was extended, the Glock aimed squarely at Dante's forehead. Two shots rang out, and Dante fell on the third step, lifeless. The gun now pointed at Fen; the barrel a mere inch from his temple. Gil was never one to hesitate, and he didn't break that pattern now. Two more shots ended Fen's life, and he crumpled to the floor.

Gil shifted his aim toward Marty, who met his gaze with an unwavering chin and no trace of fear or remorse in his eyes. Gil kept the gun trained on Marty for a count of three before flipping the barrel and offering the weapon to Marty, grip-first. Marty hesitated, leaving fifteen seconds to pass before finally taking the pistol. Gil stood there, unflinching, fully aware of the risk but harboring a history with this man that went beyond mere trust. It wasn't trust precisely, but as Gil handed over the gun, he experienced an overwhelming sense of self-destruction. Now or never, Marty, he thought. It seemed that "never" was the answer.

Marty lowered the gun and returned it to the concealed spot at the small of his back, all while keeping his eyes fixed on Gil. He warned, "You have no idea what you've just unleashed. This will haunt you, quite literally." Gil laughed, brushing off the threat. Marty continued, "I've known him for longer than I've known you, kiddo. Just look at him." When Gil's gaze remained fixed on Marty, he emphasized, "Look at him, kiddo. I've known the guy for over forty years, and he hasn't aged a day."

Gil examined Fen's lifeless face. "Imagine that. And yet, he's still dead!" With that, Gil leaned down and turned Fen's face towards him, using a cloth napkin from the nearby table to wipe off the makeup. Holding the soiled cloth up for Marty to see, he remarked, "Look at that, will you? Makeup, you fucking moron. He's wearing enough pancake to fool his own mother. This might even be undertaker quality. Unbelievable, you idiot. You never questioned it?"

Marty concealed his anger and began gathering items from the hidden room behind the bookshelf. He mentioned, "He's a rather peculiar fellow, kiddo. All those witch's ashes and skulls with horns. But that's not all." Marty found his own satchel, a striking fire-engine red with shoulder straps. He continued, "All the items we pilfered over the years, they were all for him. He was always ever our only client.

I understand that you never wanted to know who we were working for, and it was probably for the best. But everything, even that blood on our first job, was for him. And do you know what he did with it?" Marty peered out of the room and Gil shook his head, curious. Marty disclosed, "He fucking drank it. Right in front of me! Drank it. He called what we stole the Golden Blood Type, RhNull, the rarest blood type on Earth. And then, he drank it." Marty returned to the room, stuffing his red satchel with an array of valuable tools.

Gil couldn't help but notice that Marty appeared to be aging in reverse, rejuvenated before his eyes. Perhaps the older man had been leading a life filled with stress alongside the now-deceased Mr. Abaddon, master of street armies and imposter to the stars. The pretense of drug addiction seemed to serve as a front, granting Marty a semblance of street credibility for recruiting. The situation grew stranger by the minute.

As Marty rummaged through the room, muttering and grumbling to himself, the clatter of metal and the tearing of cloth reached Gil's ears. There seemed to be a note of dissatisfaction in Marty's tone. Curious, Gil called out, "What are you complaining about now?"

Marty emerged from the small room, for no apparent reason pulling the bookshelf back into its original position. He met Gil's gaze with defiance and declared, "You killed him before he could tell you about the traps."

Gil scoffed, dismissing the notion. "Traps? It's all bullshit, Marty. I'd be surprised if there's even a thousand dollars' worth of anything at the bottom of that cave." The two men chose to disagree, the matter unresolved.

The library appeared to have returned to its usual state, save for the two lifeless bodies. Gil found no incentive to conceal or erase any evidence of his actions. The remote location of the house, deep in the woods, ensured that no one would stumble upon the scene for weeks, if not months.

Gil stooped down and rifled through Dante's pockets, retrieving car keys. He then dragged Dante's body away from the library door, making way for an unobstructed exit. Rolling the maps back into their tubes, Gil slid them into his satchel.

In the wake of his actions, Gil still felt the sting of Fen Abaddon's condescending words. He moved with deliberate intent toward the corner of the room, where the glass case housed the witch's ashes. In a fit of destructive release, he knocked it over, shattering the glass bell jar and scattering shards across the floor. The wooden box inside cracked along its seam, spilling ashes in small piles along the edge of the bookshelf.

Next, he toppled the bell jar protecting the candles. But it wasn't enough. He proceeded to stomp on the candles, grinding them into the carpet with his shoe's heel. Advancing to the bell jar cradling the horned skull, he pushed it with even more force, causing it to collide with the wall and shatter. The skull rebounded and landed at his feet, one of its horns crumbling into dust upon impact. Gil picked up the skull by its eye sockets and examined it before bursting into hearty laughter.

"Marty, you're a complete imbecile, a tragic excuse for a fool. It's made of plaster of Paris." Gil held the skull out for Marty to see, and the old man's expression fell. Gil was too preoccupied with laughter to feel any sympathy for him. He flung the skull into the fireplace, where it shattered into several pieces.

A piece bounced out and landed at Marty's feet. He picked it up and examined it. He shook his head and tossed the piece back into the fireplace. He looked at Gil and said, "Are we done here?"

Gil slapped Marty on the shoulder and together they left the library and walked down the hallway to the main entrance of the house, and out the front door. It was dark.

Light from the doorway spilled out into the night. The limousine was where Dante had parked it when he brought Gil to the house. The sky was filled with stars. It was as if the city lights didn't exist where they were. And being surrounded by trees made it seem darker still.

Gil was in good spirits. Marty's face bore a smile. It was as if they'd exorcised a demon. Gil asked Marty, "Front seat or back?"

Marty opened the back door of the limo and tossed his satchel onto the back seat, then he stood aside to let Gil toss his in, too, but he kept the map tubes in hand.

"Shotgun," said Marty, and he climbed into the front passenger seat and closed the door. Gil walked the long way around the car, to the rear, completing a spot check as he went. Old habits died hard. He got to the driver's side door and stopped. He looked at the mansion they'd just left. The front door was still open and light spilled out across the driveway.

Shadows played tricks on his mind. He imagined human, and some not-so-human shapes skirting the edges of the light. He rubbed his eyes. This was a long day and he needed some sleep. He was deciding on how to attack the cave system. And fatigue was setting in, so his thoughts were all scrambled. Later, he thought. Later. He climbed into the driver's seat and slammed the door. The shadows at the edge of the light dissipated like smoke, in the glare of the headlights.

Gil tossed the tube containing the maps to Marty. "Here, make yourself useful."

"What you want me to do with this?"

"Open it, explain it in as much detail as you can, while I drive. It'll help keep me awake."

Gil put the car in Drive and pulled into the laneway. It was pitch black out the side windows of the vehicle. He put on the high beams to comfort himself in the darkness, although that made visibility worse with the branches and trees enveloping the roadway. His sleep-deprived mind played games as they careened along the lane. Faces pushed out of the branches and arms reached for the limo. Gil did not remember any of this on the way in to the house. He did remember it took a long time to get from Marine Drive to the house along this driveway. But within five minutes of driving, they reached the gate.

Gil hadn't considered this possibility. The gate remained steadfast, refusing to yield as they approached. He maneuvered the limousine to within six feet of the unyielding barrier and brought it to a halt, shifting the gear into Park. He cast an exasperated glance at Marty.

Marty returned his gaze, and with a touch of exasperation of his own, muttered, "What do you expect me to do? I can't open it."

"Damn it," Gil cursed under his breath. He left the engine idling and opened the car door, emerging into the ominous night. Marty, still seated in the passenger side, unbuckled his seatbelt but wisely chose to stay put, ready for whatever might unfold.

The limousine's headlights illuminated the gate in its entirety, revealing the same cryptic characters, though now in different, more enigmatic poses. The dancing shadows on this side of the gate played tricks on the eye, making the figures appear to writhe and contort. Exhaustion weighed heavily on Gil's shoulders. "I need sleep, and I need it badly," he mused, his voice nearly a whisper.

He cautiously approached the gate, scanning the vicinity for a keypad or any hidden mechanism that might provide an exit. No such opening presented itself.

The details on the gate's figures were nothing short of extraordinary. One depicted a naked siren, entangled in a scandalous tryst with a satyr, all the while grasping the engorged member of a horse. An ecstatic smile adorned her face, inviting all who gazed upon her. Gil, drawn to the uncanny artistry, reached out and gingerly touched her metallic belly, which felt oddly warm to the touch. As he brushed against the horse's head with his sleeve, he suddenly felt a shiver run through the beast, as if it were coming to life.

Startled, he pulled his hand away, but the woman's tiny, metal fingers clasped his pinky, their touch as sharp as a razor blade. His finger bled, and two drops fell onto the female figure's face, vanishing into the shadow that concealed her smiling mouth.

"Jesus Christ!" Gil cried out, sticking his wounded pinky into his mouth.

Marty leaped out of the passenger side, alarmed, and demanded, "What's happening?"

And just like that, the gate began to creak open of its own accord. Gil yelled, "Get in, get in!" Marty scrambled back into the limousine, and Gil rejoined him in a frantic dash. He didn't wait for the gate to fully open; as soon as it offered a slim path for the limo to escape, he floored the accelerator.

In the rear-view mirror, the gate closed behind them. Gil drove for half a block and came to a halt. His heart raced, his injured fingertip stinging fiercely, and Marty regarded him as if he was crazy.

Marty pressed, "What happened? How did you open the gate?"

Gil, bewildered and uncertain of what had just transpired, had no easy answer. "I don't know. It must have been a foot pedal or a hose I stepped on or something." He continued to nurse his wounded pinky, examining it under the overhead light. Three tiny, closely spaced pinpricks adorned the tip of his finger. The bleeding had ceased, but the stinging persisted.

Infection could be a concern, but he shoved that thought aside. "No point in worrying about tetanus now," he muttered to himself.

Marty's curiosity remained unquenched. He persisted, "Come on, Gil, tell me. What really happened?"

Gil hesitated, reluctant to spar with Marty over the deceased Mister Abaddon. He shifted the car into Drive and resumed their journey along the empty road.

Marty, his impatience palpable, inquired, "Where are we headed, kiddo?"

"City Centre Motel," Gil replied.

"What the hell? You still live there?" Marty's surprise was evident.

Gil chuckled, "I own it."

"Wow! Kiddo. You've done quite well. I'm proud to have set you on this path," Marty remarked.

"Fuck you, Marty," Gil retorted, not harboring any resentment. They continued in silence until they reached the motel's parking lot.

Marty inquired, "You got a room for me here?"

Gil sneered at Marty, "You think I'm gonna let you out of my sight? Eighty possible million dollars? You're not going anywhere. Come on." Gil exited the driver's seat, circling around to open the passenger door for Marty. Then, he unlocked the rear door and retrieved both satchels. Leading the way, Gil approached the first doorway next to the office, nodding at a young woman seated behind the counter, who waved in acknowledgment.

The motel itself was a single-story structure with twelve sleeping units. Gil unlocked the door to unit number one, flipping on the lights upon entering. Marty followed, and the room's interior exceeded his expectations. Over time, Gil had taken over three sleeping rooms, knocking down the walls between them to create a spacious twelve-hundred-square-foot, two-bedroom apartment. The layout was practical, with the kitchen sharing a wall with the office, a private entrance to the office, a living area dominated by a fifty-inch LED-HD TV, a hallway leading to two bedrooms and all the walls were adorned with artwork.

Marty's reaction was evident on his face, though he verbalized it, saying, "Wow, kiddo. I am impressed." He observed the artwork and the design with a nod and a smile. "Is this place still home to hookers and other lowlifes?"

Ignoring the question, Gil locked the apartment door, then proceeded to the living room. Marty brought a tube with him, which he opened to reveal maps that he spread across the dining table using salt and pepper shakers and a candlestick to keep them in place.

Gil examined the top map, a hand-drawn representation of Deep Cove's coastline and the local area. It depicted Vancouver from a time before urban development. Gil nodded in silent agreement with his thoughts and then rolled up the top map. Marty adjusted the shakers and the candlestick.

Examining the second map, Gil asked Marty, "Tell me what I'm looking at. You mentioned there are traps."

Marty stood beside Gil, pointing at the top of the map, explaining, "This is a crypt, and this marks the entrance to a tunnel that leads to the cave system."

Gil interrupted with a question, sensing it would be a lengthy night. "I thought Fen said the crypt was the entrance to the cave?"

Marty clarified, "The crypt is the entrance to a tunnel that leads to the cave. You see, the cave is actually at the bottom of a ravine. When this area was settled, the ravine was used as a landfill – a garbage dump – unaware of the cave beneath. The ravine was at least a hundred feet deep and maybe a quarter mile long, and a couple hundred yards wide. Abaddon bought the crypt from the family that owned it, and then he had a couple of guys empty it. I have no idea what they did with the bodies interred there. I don't want to imagine what that freak did with bones and rotten bodies."

Impatient, Gil urged Marty, "Alright, enough about that. The guy is dead; you don't have to worry about him anymore. So, they emptied the crypt. What else did they do?"

Marty continued, "They dug down to the bottom of the ravine, but they had to do it at night, really late at night, to avoid raising suspicions. Abaddon was extremely secretive, especially about this endeavor. But, you know, eighty million?" Marty raised his hands in disbelief at the vast sum.

"So, what else is on the map? Enlighten me."

"Alright, kiddo, that's the crypt," Marty repeated, tracing a line on the map representing the tunnel the men had dug at night. Then he pointed to a red circle and numerous red dots scattered across the diagram. "The red dots indicate potential traps in the cave system, according to the journal. No one has actually verified their presence, but according to the book, those are Abaddon's best guesses."

Gil inquired, "Do we know the nature of these traps? Ancient Indian rockfalls, Spanish mantraps, or things that go bump in the night?"

Marty shrugged. "You should have waited a few more minutes before you killed him. He might have been able to tell you. I was never told. I wasn't even supposed to be a part of this. You involved me when you handed me the key." Marty reached out to shake Gil's hand as if offering his gratitude. "You know, when you did that, I almost cried. It's been so long since we've seen each other, and it felt like old times, you know? Thanks for that, but seriously, no thanks for getting me into this mess, kiddo."

Gil managed to suppress his smile for about three seconds before laughing and shaking Marty's hand.

Returning his attention to the map, Gil asked, "What's at the bottom?"

Marty's excitement was palpable as he explained, "That's the goal. That's where the gold is supposedly hidden, inside a cavern. Fernando wrote that he managed to wall it in with pieces of the cart and a rockslide and locked it with a special obsidian fastener, and the key is made from the same substance. Probably a native construct of some sort."

Nodding, Gil responded, "Alright, it sounds like we have a plan. Now, let me see that key."

Marty, however, responded with concern, "What do you mean?"

"Give me the key," Gil insisted.

Marty's expression shifted to one of panic as he replied, "I don't have the key. I thought you had it."

Gil was exasperated, "Why would I have it? I gave it to you. You just said you had it."

"No, I was grateful that you trusted me with it, but you were right there when I had to give it to Mr. Abaddon. I assumed you took it back at some point. I mean, you found the car keys, and you were all over Abaddon when you wiped his makeup. I assumed," Marty stammered, visibly shaken.

Gil buried his face in his hands and muttered, "Fucks sake."


## GOING BACK


Gil felt a surge of newfound determination coursing through his veins. He sprang up from the table, his voice a raspy whisper to Marty, "Get up. Let's go." With a frantic pace, Gil rushed to the apartment door, fumbling for his keys.

Marty, frozen in a cocoon of fear, stuttered, "Why? Where are we going?" As he staggered away from the table, hesitation in his steps.

Gil's patience wore thin, and he couldn't contain himself, yelling, "Back!"

"Back? Back where?" Marty stammered, his voice quivering.

"Back. To retrieve the God-damned key," Gil exclaimed, gesturing wildly, urging Marty into action. He lunged forward, seizing Marty's arm and dragging him towards the door. "Move." With a swift motion, Gil locked the apartment door behind them and slid into the limo's driver's seat, Marty joining him on the passenger side.

Gil set the tone, "First, we're going to pick up my truck at the Sunrise and abandon the limo. You'll drive it, and then we'll return to Abaddon's to get the key. Understand?"

When Marty's response wasn't immediate, Gil barked, "Do you understand?"

Marty nodded, teary-eyed and sleepy. He replied, "Yes, I understand, kiddo. I'm catching up, I promise."

"Good. Buckle up. What time is it?"

Marty glanced at his watch. "It's half past three."

Gil wasted no time, "Right. Dawn's not far off. Let's get moving." The engine roared to life, and they sped off into the night.

Arriving at the Sunrise Tavern, Gil found his truck exactly where he'd left it. Marty transitioned from the limo to the truck, and with a swift turn of the key, the engine rumbled to life. Gil climbed into the passenger seat. Marty drove down the alley. Passing the dumpster that once held a nearly dead Dante, Gil pondered the life-altering decisions that had led him to this fateful night. Not a good man, not a kind man, just the sort of person Fenriz Abaddon had described him as—a perfect match for the devil's intentions.

Their journey to Marine Drive took about twenty minutes. Approaching their destination, they spotted the ominous flashing blue and red lights of a police car in the distance. A police car blocked access to the estate, and the gate stood wide open. Marty slowed down, feigning casual curiosity, passing the obstacle.

At the next corner, Marty turned right. They parked beneath a tree, hidden from prying eyes by the cover of darkness, in front of another mansion-like residence. All the nearby houses remained shrouded in nighttime oblivion, offering little chance of being noticed. Marty killed the engine and turned off the lights. They got out and walked back to the intersection, to observe.

Marty couldn't hold back his confusion any longer. "How did they get here so quickly? Are you sure they were both dead?"

Gil, his neck tense and mind racing, rubbed the back of his head. "Two slugs in Dante and another couple in

Abaddon, there's no way they survived. I felt it when I touched them. This doesn't make sense."

Marty posed the inevitable question, "What do we do now?"

As the two men huddled in the dark, Gil formulated a plan. "Get back in the truck, hand me my balaclava from behind the seat. Here's what you'll do." Their conversation remained hushed, safeguarded by the shadows and the massive oak tree obscuring them.

Following Gil's instructions, Marty returned along Marine Drive, feigning curiosity once more when he reached the police activity at the gate. This time, he pulled over, stepping out of the truck. A police officer emerged from the cruiser, his Mag Light casting an eerie glow, revealing Marty's face.

"Good evening, officer," Marty greeted with feigned innocence.

"Sir, get back in your vehicle," the officer ordered, illuminating Marty's form with his flashlight.

Unseen by the officer but visible to Marty, Gil, concealed by his balaclava and dark clothing, crept from the shadows, darting along the hedge before vanishing into Fenriz Abaddon's estate. As soon as Gil disappeared from view, Marty fell in line with the officer's commands. "Sorry, sir. Just curious. You don't see much action in this part of town. Didn't mean to bother you."

He re-entered the truck, turned left at the next corner, executed a slick three-point U-turn, and parked at a strategic corner, his eyes glued to Abaddon's gate, waiting in suspense.

Once through the gate, Gil knew better than to run along the gravel; the crunching underfoot would echo like a gunshot at three in the morning. He hugged the road's edge, utilizing tall grass to muffle his footfalls. It was remarkable how the roadway transformed when traversed on foot as opposed to behind the wheel of a car.

When he was reasonably certain he'd distanced himself from the gate and rounded a gentle bend in the lane, he abandoned the grassy cover, hastening his steps along the dirt and gravel path. The surrounding underbrush, possibly twigs and branches, tugged at his clothing as he dashed past. Or so he tried to convince himself, refusing to let his mind conjure phantoms and demons lurking in the dark.

The lane ultimately led to a small parking area near the front entrance of the house. There, two police cars and a coroner's station-wagon-style ambulance had been haphazardly parked, their flashing blue and red lights piercing the quiet night. The headlights pointed aimlessly into the surrounding woods, casting eerie shadows. The front door was wide open, and a police officer stood on the doorstep, scribbling into his notepad. Gil concealed himself behind a sizable bush beside one of the police cars.

Two attendants wheeled a gurney, concealed beneath a shroud, out of the front door and along the gravel path toward the rear of the ambulance. Gil knew it was a lifeless form, given the meticulous draping of the sheet and the securing straps. They loaded the gurney into the back of the ambulance, headfirst, and anchored it firmly to the floor to prevent any jostling during transit. The second gurney was promptly taken into the house, accompanied by the police officer.

Gil didn't wait for an invitation. He darted around the bush and knelt beside the police car, keeping a watchful eye on the front door. There was no visible movement. He estimated he had a mere three or four minutes before they reappeared with the second body, be it living or dead. He sprinted to the back of the ambulance and slipped inside.

Gil slid alongside the gurney, reaching the head and drawing back the shroud. Damn. It was Dante. He had hoped for Fen, in the hopes of finding the key. Gil patted the deceased man's forehead in apology for killing him and gently draped the sheet back over his face. Trapped inside the ambulance, he anxiously pondered his options. If the attendants returned now, he would be apprehended. He silently exited the rear of the ambulance and retreated to the shelter of the bush.

His timing was impeccable. The two attendants emerged onto the front step, wheeling the second gurney. The first attendant, positioned at the feet, paused as he passed through the doorway. Gil observed the police officer conversing with the attendant still at the head. Their words were inaudible, but he couldn't see if the sheet was draped or not, signaling life or death. They stood there, engaged in their conversation, seemingly for an eternity.

At last, the attendants emerged from the house into the parking area. The shroud remained draped, covering the entire length of the gurney. Abaddon was most certainly deceased. Gil breathed a sigh of relief. Thank goodness. Curse Marty and his ghost stories. A gunshot wound to the temple was unquestionably fatal. It had to be. Fuck you, Marty, for planting these thoughts in my head.

The attendants shoved the second gurney into the back of the ambulance, beside Dante's lifeless form. They slammed the rear door shut, with one of them returning to the driver's side and the other re-entering the house, with the police officer following. The ambulance's engine roared to life, and the attendant behind the wheel lit a cigarette, taking his focus from any potential threat in the back. Gil moved like a shadow. He silently cracked the rear door just enough to slide his narrow frame inside the ambulance. He pulled the door to the frame without fully closing it. He slid into position between the gurneys.

He ran his hands along Fen's lifeless body, probing for the elusive key underneath the shroud or concealed in his pockets. Unfortunately, his search yielded nothing. The securing straps on the gurney were strategically positioned to hinder any movement or access. One at the shins, the other at the shoulders, with the sheet draping in between and at either end. Any pockets lay concealed beneath the straps. Gil gathered the shroud to facilitate a more thorough exploration.

In that critical moment, the passenger-side door swung open, and the second attendant climbed into the ambulance, tossing a black satchel onto the floor between his seat and the driver's. Gil instinctively dived under the shroud, curling up as tightly as possible. He managed to draw his legs beneath the gurney, nestled between the wheels at one end, and his head and shoulders concealed at the other. His ploy went unnoticed; neither attendant made any remarks.

The driver said, "You took your sweet time. Did they tell you anything?"

The second attendant appeared annoyed as he responded, "Get rid of that God-damned cigarette, would you?" He waved his hands in front of his face to clear the smoky haze, rolling down his window.

The driver flicked his cigarette butt out the window and asked, "Happy now?"

The second attendant replied, "Yes, thanks."

"So, what did they say?"

"The cop told me he was doing his usual drive-by for Mister Abaddon, a routine check. He saw the front door wide open, lights on, no one in sight. He went inside and discovered them dead in the library. It was like a game of Clue." Both attendants shared a chuckle at that.

"Yeah, a bloody game of Clue. 'I killed Mister Abaddon in the library with the candlestick.'" Both attendants reveled in their jests as the ambulance began to move.

Gil fought off panic. While the two men indulged in their Clue banter, he slid his hands beneath the shroud and through Fen's pockets methodically, leaving nothing to chance. He couldn't afford to second-guess himself. It all hinged on thoroughness. Front pants pocket, nearest to him, revealed nothing. The rear pocket, still empty. Gil reached across the body under the shroud, exploring the front and back pockets on the far side, and found nothing. He encountered Fen's jacket, still intact beneath the shroud. He located the front pocket on this side, empty as well, and then reached across to explore the other. Nothing. Damn it. He reached upward, delving into the inner jacket pocket.

When the ambulance moved, the gurneys rocked back and forth from the weight of the bodies they carried. They were anchored to the floor so they didn't roll, as the ambulance proceeded into the darkness and up the laneway. The crunch of the gravel under the vehicle's tires along with the static from their dispatch-radio, covered any noise Gil was making in the back. The two attendants were still laughing. They'd moved on to dick jokes.

The ambulance glided toward the gate, its headlights casting eerie shadows in the night. A solitary police officer stood guard – his figure illuminated by the ambulance as it came to a stop. The driver lowered the radio's volume, muffling the static noise that had been filling the air.

The cop leaned towards the window and greeted the driver, his words laced with a hint of familiarity and jest, "Hey Schlomo. How's it hanging?" Gil couldn't discern whether the officer was using the driver's name or offering a subtle insult.

Schlomo responded in kind, "I'm good, Officer Dickwad." Gil realized it was likely just banter exchanged between fellow first-responders.

Officer Dickwad chuckled and inquired, "You get anything?"

Schlomo, clearly not taking offense, retorted, "What kind of a question is that? Do we look like thieves to you?" The attendant patted the black satchel on the seat between him and the passenger. A wry smile on his face.

Laughter filled the air as they shared a moment of camaraderie. Again, the officer laughed, "Sure as shit, you do." Their shared laughter echoed in the night.

Meanwhile, Gil meticulously re-searched the jacket, desperate to find another inside pocket. His efforts were in vain. He patted Fen's lifeless body, searching every pocket from top to bottom, but found nothing.

The cop, still chuckling, asked, "Are my buddies getting their goodies back there?"

Schlomo replied, "Far as I could see. You should get down there before all the good shit is gone. But, be careful. Some of that stuff is fake. I don't know why we believed in this guy for so long."

"Fake? From Abaddon? That's surprising," they all found humor in the absurdity.

The ambulance driver requested the cop to move his vehicle, saying, "Want to move that thing so we can get out of here?"

The officer had a different idea, "I was thinking I give the bodies the once over, just to see if they had anything of value on them." Gil's heart skipped a beat.

Schlomo interjected, "You think we didn't think about that. Your buddy got there first, so the deeds already done."

Gil's hopes dwindled as he realized someone had beaten him to the key. One of the officers had it or had dismissed it as inconsequential. Everything seemed to be going wrong that night.

The cop grumbled, "Ah, that asshole. Yeah, you're right. Latecomers get what's left. I'll get out of your way. Later Schlomo." His footsteps faded away on the gravel, then clicked on the pavement as he departed. The police car's engine roared to life, its headlights briefly illuminating the ambulance's interior, making Gil duck down. The ambulance moved forward, then stopped, and the driver got out.

A hushed conversation ensued between the driver and the cop. "You sure he's dead?"

"Yeah, this time for sure. Two in the temple. He ain't coming back from that."

"Good. And good riddance. Take care Schlomo."

"You too Dickwad." The gravel crunched as the police car drove through the gates.

The sound of the police car's engine faded with distance, and Gil realized the cop was heading back to the house to search for anything valuable, now that the owner was confirmed dead.

The gates creaked on their hinges and slammed shut as they closed. The driver's footsteps echoed as he approached the ambulance. The interior light came on as the driver opened the door. Gil timed his escape at the same time. He pushed the rear door open when the front door opened and he slammed it in concert with the driver. He rolled across six feet of pavement and laid in the shadow created at the foot of the gate.

The attendant in the passenger seat wondered aloud, "You hear that?"

Gil imagined their puzzled faces peering backwards, into the ambulance. He remained still.

After a brief pause, the attendant dismissed it, "Nothing, I guess. Let's go."

The ambulance pulled onto Marine Drive, its flashing lights now engaged, but no sirens, as there was no need to hurry with their lifeless cargo.

Gil remained hidden in the shadows until the flashing lights disappeared from view. He then crawled to the driveway's side and sat in the shadows, gathering his thoughts. Eventually, he walked down the block to where Marty awaited him in the truck. He removed his balaclava, not wanting to attract attention from any locals who might pass by, though it was unlikely at this early hour.

Entering the truck's passenger seat, Gil closed the door, and Marty jolted awake, startled. "Christ, you scared the shit out of me."

"You fell asleep?" Gil couldn't hide his astonishment. "I was over there with cops and everything, risking it all, and you were asleep?" He tossed his balaclava into the space behind the driver's seat.

Marty inquired, "Did you get the key?"

Gil reached over and turned the key in the ignition, starting the engine. "No. I think one of the cops has it."

The truck's engine roared to life, and Gil gestured for Marty to drive. "Take us home."

Marty was practically bursting with excitement. "Are we done, then? No key means we're done, right?"

"Take us home. Let me think." Marty shifted into Drive.

As they approached a stop sign at Marine Drive, Marty checked both ways before turning left. Under the sodium streetlight, the truck's side displayed remnants of its former life, "The Locksmith" emblazoned in faded, bold letters, with the O and C forming a lock. The lower-left corner still bore the name and number of the owner: Gil T. Proprietor. But as the truck moved away from the light, it returned to its matte-black guise, concealing its past.

Marty guided the vehicle back to the City Center Motel. No one was present at the front desk when they arrived. Gil unlocked his apartment door, and they entered. Handing the key to Marty, he locked the door from the inside.

Exhausted, Gil announced, "I'm going to bed. Make yourself at home. There's beer and food in the fridge. Help yourself."

Marty asked one final question, "You know you're a fucking locksmith, right?"

Gil, his fatigue showing, furrowed his brow, "What?"

Marty grabbed a beer from the fridge and took a sip. "So, what if we don't have the key? A key just opens a lock. You're a fucking locksmith. Do you even need the key?"

A smile slowly crept across Gil's face as the realization hit him. "You're a fucking genius, Marty. Did I ever tell you that?"

Marty raised his beer in a salute, "I know. You don't have to say it."

"Goodnight, genius."


## THE MAUSOLEUM


The next morning, Marty carried two cups of coffee to the dining table, the strategic hub of operations in Gil's clandestine hideout. In the dimly lit room, the two men huddled over an array of meticulously spread maps.

Marty leaned back in his chair, his furrowed brow betraying a sense of impending danger. Gil lifted his gaze from the enigmatic papers and raised a quizzical eyebrow in Marty's direction. "What's the prob, slob?" he inquired, adopting a casual stance that concealed the gravity of their situation.

Marty took a contemplative sip of his coffee before speaking, his voice a mere whisper of concern. "I can't help but wish you'd given Abaddon ten more minutes to unravel the intricacies of those traps. That's the 'prob'."

Gil shrugged off the concern. He returned his attention to the maps, his finger tracing the ancient cave system's twists and turns. "How bad can it be? A lone man in the fifteenth century, setting traps in a cave – it's about as low-tech as it gets. If they were set fifty years ago, maybe I'd be on edge. But this... this is nothing."

Marty sighed once more, the weight of undisclosed information pressing upon him. He sipped his coffee, and the words tumbled out, each more revealing than the last. "He wasn't alone."

Gil's probing finger froze mid-trace, and he locked eyes with Marty, sensing a concealed truth. With a deep breath, Gil cautiously inquired, "The woman?"

Marty shook his head, shrouding the mystery in further layers. "No, not just Fernando and the woman."

"Then who?" Gil demanded his curiosity piqued.

Marty, still concealing crucial details, sipped his coffee again and finally revealed the hidden complexity of their mission. "According to Fen, the priest embarked on his journey with a retinue of natives from the woman's tribe."

The revelation struck Gil like a thunderbolt. "Right, right, but still, fifteenth century?"

Marty replied, his voice veiled in the shadows of subterfuge, "Fen has known for a long time. He invested substantial resources in translating the journal and surveying the properties, but he never once breathed a word about the traps. He shared the story of the priest's journey and the entourage of men that accompanied him. And the whole 'meeting with the devil' thing." Both men rolled their eyes. "Alright forget that part, but he wasn't alone."

Gil grappled with this newfound complexity, the gravity of their mission deepening with each revelation. "So, these traps may be more intricate than we initially believed."

"Yep." Marty finished his coffee and brought his cup to the sink. He ran the tap and started washing the dishes. He continued, "The story is much more elaborate than you heard at the house. Fernando and his team ran into all kinds of trouble. Other tribes not liking trespassers on their hunting grounds. Wild animals. Wild waters. All kinds of stuff. You probably should have asked to see the journal translations. There was so much more to know, kiddo."

Gil threw his hands up, in surrender, "Alright, so sorry I killed the man ten minutes too soon. I saw my opportunity and I took it. Christ, Marty, I was pretty sure Dante was going to kill me. Maybe both of us."

With the tension between them escalating, Marty ventured to set the record straight. "I was never in danger, Gil. I've known Dante for years, long before Fen had him rescued from that dumpster – the one you left him in by the way. You had reason to be concerned, but not me."

Gil leaned back, folding his arms as they reverted to their established roles. Mentor and mentee, master and apprentice, with two decades of separation vanishing in an instant. Marty's smile softened, a gesture of reassurance. "Relax, kiddo. We need to focus on the task at hand. We don't know who might have the key to the treasure or if the police or someone else is onto it. I always assumed that if Abaddon told me, he might as well have told the whole world."

Gil, reminded of their shared history, finally conceded. "You're right, Marty. Let's not waste time on old grudges. We need to get moving."

As they resumed their planning, Gil suggested, "We're going to need some capable people for this thing. Maybe some of the men we've seen down at the Sunrise?

Skilled, unafraid of risk, and, uh, well, expendable. Should we ask Stan?"

Marty offered an alternative, his tone infused with authority. "Sure, if you want to involve Stan, but I have connections to a network of guys and gals who could fit the bill. I used to recruit for Abaddon, forming what he called his 'Army.' I know some skilled expendables."

With an understanding reached, Marty reinforced the importance of their partnership. "Besides, if we involve Stan, he'll demand a share. I want half of whatever we find."

Gil, momentarily taken aback by the equal split, processed the information and then surrendered, "Sorry for thinking it would be all mine, a hundred percent. You're right, and who knows, this may all be a wild goose chase, anyway. If that's the case, we'll split nothing two ways. Equal partners it is."

Marty extended his soapy-sudsy hand to Gil, sealing the agreement. "That's the spirit, kiddo."

As they readied themselves for the mission ahead, the roles were solidified. Gil, with an air of determination, chuckled at their mutual understanding. Both men laughed, sharing a moment of camaraderie. Marty tossed a hand towel to Gil, and they prepared to embark on their enigmatic journey.

In their truck, enroute to the south end of town, Marty deftly utilized his cell phone, summoning a group of trusted individuals. By the time they reached Mount View Cemetery, they had secured three reliable and resourceful comrades. Though only one side of the conversations was audible, Marty's responses remained consistent:

"Hey, it's Marty... Yeah, I heard the news too... I've got a job. Thought you might want in... The right man can earn a couple of grand for a few days' work... That's the spirit, I'll be in touch... Probably tomorrow, unless I need you tonight... No, no guns... Okay, wait for my call."

With the task force assembled, Marty shared vital information with Gil. "Everyone knows that Abaddon's dead, but no one knows by who or how."

Gil acknowledged the progress with a nod. "That's good to hear. Sounds like you've got your team lined up."

"Yeah, it's all good."

The cemetery occupied a picturesque location on the east side of south Vancouver, once a landfill that had been filled in and covered with a layer of dirt. From certain vantage points, one could glimpse distant mountains to the north. The graveyard was well-kept, and at this early hour, few visitors roamed the grounds.

Gil eventually located the crypt he sought, and its impressive size took him by surprise. From a distance, it had appeared unremarkable, but up close, it resembled a suburban bungalow with an attached shed. Gil turned to Marty, puzzled by what he saw. "Is that really a garage?"

Marty replied knowingly, "It must be. They dug a tunnel from the crypt down through the landfill to access the caves. Having a garage would have been an excellent way to conceal the removal of dirt."

Gil questioned the logic behind digging a tunnel if they could have not immediately searched for the caves and the gold. Marty, however, reminded him of Abaddon's eccentricities and his unsettling rituals. "The man was a whack-job, and after witnessing him drinking that blood, I never questioned anything he did."

Determined, Gil declared, "I'm going in."

Marty jumped out of the truck, offering half-hearted assurance, "I'll stay out here and keep watch."

Gil couldn't help but mock, "You fucking coward."

Marty asserted, "I'll keep watch."

Gil drove the truck into the garage, closing the door behind him. Inside, he reached for his flashlight and ventured toward a secondary entrance within the garage. The flashlight cast a wide beam of light, revealing a chamber with walls lined from floor to ceiling with small niches for urns. At the far end, he noticed an elaborate entryway leading outside, adorned with intricate sculptures of human figures in various sensual and exotic entanglements, similar to the gate at Fen's estate but even more finely detailed. Gil cautiously avoided the gate, fearing that the figures might reach out and grab him in their sensuous poses, his nerves already on edge.

On the opposite wall, Gil counted thirty-two marble cubby-holes designed for urns. One niche, large enough to contain a casket, near the far-left corner of the room, stood open, its marble face smashed and scattered in pieces beside it. A lavish casket, adorned with brass and mahogany fixtures, rested against the wall. Scratches on the floor revealed that the casket had been dragged from the niche. A trail of dirt extended from the niche to the garage entrance, indicating the path to the tunnel that Abaddon's men had excavated.

Gil inspected the hole in the wall, where he noticed a jagged edge. His flashlight's feeble beam couldn't penetrate even to the back of the alcove, making it impossible to discern what had been done by Abaddon's people.

Doubts gnawed at him, and he whispered to himself, "Get a grip." Pushing aside fear, he inched closer to the gloomy opening. Gil decided to crawl into the niche to investigate further. The space felt cramped, and the stale smell of dirt and decay made his skin crawl. After squirming along about five feet, the floor ended abruptly. Stretching out, he shone his light into the hole but found no visible bottom. He struggled against claustrophobia and paranoia, reminding himself that it couldn't be bottomless.

As he backed out of the cavity, a sudden grip on his collar froze him in place. Panic set in as he wriggled, desperately trying to free himself, but the grip from behind was unrelenting. He feared being thrust into the gaping hole, and his efforts to break free intensified. The collar of his jacket tore slightly before his unseen assailant released him. Gasping for breath, he fell to the ground, his ragged breaths causing small clouds of dust to rise. A small patch of cloth dangled from a jagged piece of marble at the opening.

He retreated from the niche, sat with his back to the casket, and took deep breaths, silently cursing Marty for sowing such delusions in him. He'd never been the type to panic in any situation, but the incident had shaken him. Gradually, he calmed his racing pulse, bringing his anxiety back under control. He touched his neck, waiting for his heart rate to return to normal. After a moment, he decided to carry on.

Exiting the crypt, Gil locked the garage door and returned to the truck. Marty was already in the passenger seat. Concerned, he asked, "What happened to your jacket?"

With a curt "Shut up" in response, Gil drove them back to the motel in tense silence.

# THE CRYPT

Gil and Marty sat at the battered dining table, positioned strategically between the living area and the shabby kitchen. Gil wore the bored expression of a taskmaster assessing a trio of would-be assistants, while Marty, his loyal partner in this shadowy enterprise, wore a knowing smile.

Gil couldn't help but draw comparisons to a carnival midway, where oddities awaited within a freak show tent. He leaned in close, his voice a conspiratorial whisper in Marty's ear, "Are these the best you could come up with?"

Marty leaned back, returning the smile to Gil, and then shifted his gaze toward the three anxious individuals who stood before them. With a thumbs-up gesture, he encouraged them to relax, though one of the men, a chap with mismatched socks, briefly dared to sit on the arm of an easy chair. That recklessness drew a scowl from Gil, and the man jumped back to his feet.

The three men, to Gil's dismay, were a far cry from the recruits he had expected. They exuded the air of lowlifes, the sort that haunted the darker corners of the Sunrise Tavern. Their disheveled appearances, one with two different colored socks, another lacking socks entirely, betrayed the absence of honest labor for a considerable period. They presented a bizarre mix of body types, defying classification.

Though unimpressed, Gil recognized the value these men brought to the mission. They were, in essence, his canaries in the mine—essential for a specific purpose. He decided to cast aside his initial scowl, treating them as the valuable assets they were.

"Gentlemen," Gil began, prompting the three men to puff their chests out slightly, "Thank you for coming today. We have a gig, and each of you will play a crucial role in its success. It all starts now."

The first portly man, Basic, spoke up, expressing his honor at working with "The Locksmith." The other two men nodded vigorously in agreement – their eyes gleaming with anticipation. Basic then inquired about the job.

Before proceeding, Gil asked the men to introduce themselves, and they offered their street names: Basic, Stretch, and Arbuckle. Arbuckle, in particular, went on a rambling explanation of his nickname, only ceasing when Gil gave a pointed "Ahem." Stretch offered a consoling nudge to Arbuckle.

Marty, sensing the need to steer the conversation back on course, took charge of explaining the mission. He and Gil skillfully omitted any mention of a treasure or Abaddon, keeping the men focused on one task at a time. Their initial objective was to acquire the necessary gear, with headlamps, steel-toed boots, and leather gloves provided by Gil and Marty. Once their hunger was addressed with grilled cheese sandwiches and coffee, they were ready to depart for the cemetery in the afternoon.

Driving the truck, Gil was flanked by Marty in the passenger seat, while the three men sat in the back, their conversation hushed. Stretch playfully donned his headlamp, jokingly comparing himself to a miner. Arbuckle, however, was puzzled by a sign at a bar that read "No Minors" until Stretch explained the distinction between "miner" and "minor."

A scuffle ensued in the back of the truck, and the three men engaged in a shouting match. Gil allowed it for a short time, hoping they would stop on their own, but when they persisted, he abruptly braked at a red light, sending them tumbling into the back of the front seats. That effectively silenced them for the remainder of the journey.

Upon reaching the cemetery, Gil drove the truck into the garage beside the mausoleum, and Basic closed the garage door behind them. Stretch and Arbuckle began unloading ropes and equipment under Marty's watchful gaze, stacking everything near the opened casket niche.

Gathering everyone in the main crypt room, Gil distributed walkie-talkies, emphasizing the use of channel nine and the importance of omitting names and locations from their conversations.

Arbuckle playfully tested the rule, by triggering the call button, "This is me, is that you?" But he and Stretch ceased their joking when they noticed Gil's stern expression.

Marty anchored a rope to the mausoleum's gate and tied a flashlight to the other end. Positioned at the niche's entrance, he waited for Gil to join him with more equipment. With an exchange of glances, Marty handed Gil the torch. Gil moved to the edge of the alcove, laying on his belly, and Marty secured his ankles.

Marty offered some words of encouragement, and a playful exchange followed. Arbuckle, ever eager to join in on the camaraderie, laughed, but the laughter quickly died as everyone's eyes fixed on him. Gil's assurance brimming, he peered into the abyss and dropped the flashlight into the darkness. As the rope slipped through his fingers like silk, he called back to Marty, "How much you give me?"

"A hundred feet," Marty yelled into the niche, their journey into the unknown now fully underway.

Gil looked over the edge of the tunnel. An odor, a blend of aged refuse and centuries-old decay, rose from the abyss below. With each passing moment, the light at the rope's end dwindled, shrinking to a mere pinprick as more line played out. Then, after about half the cord was let loose, it slackened, a subtle sign that the flashlight had either found the tunnel's bottom or caught up on a hidden ledge.

Gil meticulously retrieved the slack, allowing it to fall in a calculated rhythm, attempting to jolt the rope free if it clung to a lip. Satisfied that the flashlight had finally found its resting place at the tunnel's floor, he took a glance over the edge, only to discern a faint trail of light etching the bottom of this mysterious abyss, too distant to reveal any details. He hollered back to Marty, "How much line you got left? I think we've hit the floor."

Marty scrutinized the rope and reported, "There's about ten or fifteen feet left, which means we're only eighty-five feet deep."

Gil welcomed this assessment. "Pull me out," he shouted. Marty enlisted the aid of Basic, and together they pulled Gil out. Gil sprang up, dusting himself off, and thanked Basic with a firm slap on the shoulder. "Fetch the rope ladders," he ordered. Basic quickly grabbed Stretch, and they darted to the truck, returning with the hefty, coiled rope ladder. The ladder was an unwieldy burden, necessitating two men to carry it.

Marty gestured for them to secure the ladder's end to the same gate that held the other rope. They unrolled the ladder, and it fit snugly into the crevice. Gil took charge, dragging the coiled ladder into the murky abyss. He balanced the coil at the precipice, rolled onto his side, ensuring that no part of his limbs came into contact with the now uncoiled portion.

Once ready, he bellowed, "Fire in the hole!" and flung the rope ladder over the edge. The weight of the ladder unfurled it into a taut line that struck the ceiling. Had any part of Gil been in its path, it could have resulted in a broken arm or neck, or worse.

The ladder descended, creating a symphony of clatters and crashes that reverberated through the tunnel. It began as a deafening roar, echoing down the shaft, but after a few seconds, the noise dulled into a low growl before finally falling silent. Gil crept to the edge and peered down; the dim light still persisted but was partly veiled by the ladder's end. He yelled once more, "Pull me out!"

In the crypt, Gil gathered the men. "We're going in. Marty's going to remain above ground. The rest of you and I are heading down to explore. Our mission is to locate the entrance to a cave. Find that, and we can call it a day. That's what we're here for, gentlemen. Any questions?"

Marty would remain above while the rest descended the rope ladder to search for an entrance to a cave. Simple and direct. No mention of treasures or Abaddon. A plan focused on one task at a time.

Basic and Stretch listened attentively, while Arbuckle fiddled with his headlamp and unintentionally diverted attention, flashing its beam across the walls of the crypt. Gil's swift reprimand, an open-handed slap on the forehead, prompted Arbuckle to make it known he had a question, raising his hand like a schoolchild.

Exercising infinite patience, Gil asked Arbuckle gently, "Do you have a question?"

"Sorry boss. Yeah. I have a question." Arbuckle scanned his friends faces. "But I forget."

The situation evolved into a shared bout of laughter, providing a brief respite from the mounting tension. Despite the chuckles, Arbuckle seemed perpetually befuddled, but joined in the laughter. His innocence was out of place in this room.

Gil, having endured a most undignified journey across the floor, twice over, dusted himself off, again. He strode toward the niche's entrance, his voice steady as he addressed the assembled men. "Arbuckle, you're up first, followed by Stretch, then me, and our last man down is Basic."

Arbuckle, with a dubious look etched on his face, inquired, "Why am I first?"

Gil approached Arbuckle, casually draping his arm around the big man's shoulders and guiding him to a heap of gear. He handed Arbuckle a pair of rugged leather gloves and deftly secured a headlamp on his head. Gil's response was matter-of-fact, "Because, my dear Arbuckle, you're the one I'm most concerned about losing his footing. And trust me, I'd rather not be beneath you if that were to happen. So, get your behind into that hole and down that ladder."

Reluctantly, Arbuckle prepared to crawl headfirst into the niche, but Gil intervened. "No, you'll need to crawl backward. That way, your feet lead the way down the hole. Otherwise, you'd be going down headfirst."

Tears welled in Arbuckle's eyes, his hands trembling as he donned the gloves. "Stretch, man, I'm scared."

Stretch offered Arbuckle a comforting embrace. "I'm scared too, Arby. But you've got this. Go ahead, and I'll be right behind you, or I guess, on top of you."

Arbuckle's emotional state was deteriorating, his lower lip quivering uncontrollably. Basic, growing impatient, interjected, "Come on, man. Suck it up! You're making a shit-ton of money for this. Get in the fucking hole!"

Stretch shot a disapproving glare at Basic. "Back off, B. There's no need to make it worse." He turned his attention to Arbuckle and said, "Slow and steady wins the race, Arby. Slow and steady. Just keep saying it."

Arbuckle, despite his fear, began to back into the niche and inched toward the tunnel's edge. The other men watched intently as he negotiated his way into the hole and commenced his descent. When his head and shoulders were level with the floor, he called out to Stretch, "You coming, man?"

Stretch replied, "Absolutely, right behind you. Take it slow, okay? I'll see you at the bottom."

Arbuckle's head and shoulders disappeared into the inky blackness, his voice muttering to himself, "Slow and steady...slow and steady...see you at the bottom...slow..."

Stretch followed suit, backing his legs into the niche. He flashed a smile at Gil. "Wish me luck." He gradually crawled to the tunnel's edge, legs dangling, and just before he descended, he looked up at Gil, who was next in line. "Don't be too hard on Arby. He's not all there, but he's got a big heart."

Gil nodded in silence, offering encouragement as Stretch's head vanished into the abyss. Gil took his place and inched backward toward the rope ladder. He let his feet hang over the edge, the ladder swaying gently as the men below navigated from rung to rung. Basic awaited his turn, and Gil advised him, "Wait ten seconds before you start. We don't want you stepping on me if these guys stall."

"Sure thing, boss. I'll give you some time," Basic affirmed as Gil clung to the rope ladder and began his descent.

Gil's headlamp cast flickering light on the tunnel walls. The tunnel's tight confines unexpectedly evoked more feelings of claustrophobia. At least there were no ominous hands grabbing at him this time. His exhalations reverberated off the wall before him as he descended one rung at a time. When he peered downward, he observed Stretch's light bouncing off the tunnel walls. Arbuckle's lamp remained obscured by Stretch's bulk.

The ladder swayed continually, though it lay almost flush against the tunnel wall. To reach the next rung, Gil had to nudge the landfill wall with the toe of his boot. In some areas, the ground felt soft, in others squishy. As his face drew near a section of the tunnel wall that had been disturbed, the stench overwhelmed him. In some spots, the filth oozed onto the ladder rungs, a moment when he was grateful for his nearly waterproof leather gloves. Next time, he resolved, he'd bring rubber gloves.

Above him, Basic was tackling the ladder. Any faint light that filtered down from above was now entirely eclipsed by Basic's presence. Gil suppressed any negative emotions and day-dreamed on what eighty million dollars might look like, if it were all piled into one room.

Below Gil, something was happening. Someone was shouting, and it could only be Arbuckle, Gil surmised. The man was celebrating his descent, and Gil allowed him his moment of jubilation. Arbuckle was hollering Stretch's name, exultant. Stretch, however, implored him to be quiet, but Arbuckle showed no signs of stopping. The rope beneath Gil's feet slackened as Stretch reached the bottom and left the ladder, rendering Gil's descent more challenging. Without the ladder bearing any weight below him, finding the next rung became problematic as it swung unpredictably. Gil resolved to steady the ladder for Basic when his turn arrived.

Looking downward, Gil spotted the beams of light from both men below, their beams dancing in the now-expansive space. When Gil was within twenty feet of the bottom, the tunnel widened, and the ladder no longer scraped against the walls. Instead, it swung freely in open space. He called down to Stretch, "Hey, stabilize the ladder for me." Stretch grabbed the ladder's base and applied his weight, restricting the ladder's lateral movement.

It was evident to Gil that the landfill was far less stable than natural dirt or rock. They would need to remain vigilant for potential falls or even a cave-in.

Gil, fixated on his descent and distracted, failed to move his hands quickly enough, and Basic's foot landed squarely on his fingers. Gil lost his grip with one hand, and in the midst of a step, he tumbled off the ladder. He couldn't help but exclaim, "Shit." But his words offered no comfort.

Gil's arms flailed, searching desperately for something to grasp, but there was nothing to hold onto. He couldn't press against the tunnel walls, which had grown too distant to touch from the ladder. He fell backward, contemplating his impending death. Right here, right now, he pondered. He braced himself for the cavern floor's sudden stop.

As he tumbled, his left foot remained ensnared on a ladder rung, its tension causing the toe of his boot to jam into the rung's loop. His boot's tip caught on the top rung, saving him from breaking his neck, while his heel slipped over the next rung. He dangled upside down, the rungs pressing into his skin, the only damage suffered being to his pride. Ten feet above the cavern floor, Gil's head swung back and forth.

From above, Basic called out, "Boss, are you okay? Was that your hand I stepped on? Jesus, man, I'm sorry. Are you alright?"

Gil couldn't help but laugh, his amusement infectious, as Arbuckle joined in, regardless of whether he understood why. "Yeah, you clumsy shit. I'm fine. For now." Gil hung upside down for a few moments longer, all three headlamps trained on him, one from above and two from below. The walls sparkled in the beam from his headlamp. Very curious.

Gil shouted, "Hey, Arby, climb up this rope and help me free my leg."

Arbuckle willingly obliged. "Sure thing, boss. I've got you." Arbuckle ascended the ladder while Stretch steadied it below. Arbuckle positioned himself face-to-face with Gil, his hand gripping Gil's shoulder, pushing upward. Gil cooperated with Arbuckle's assistance and used his own strength to hoist himself back onto the ladder. It took a minute to extract his foot from the rungs. Once Gil was making progress, Arbuckle descended. When Gil reached the bottom, he shook Arbuckle's hand in gratitude.

A minute later, Basic arrived at the cavern's floor.

## THE TUNNEL DOWN

The quartet of men huddled together, their shadows cast in eerie, shifting patterns by the dim beams of their headlamps. The rocky floor of the cavern was littered with patches of displaced dirt, remnants of the landfill overhead. The walls, constructed from the same ancient stone as the ground, reached a height of around twenty feet before melding into the landfill. Mysterious, twinkling minerals sparkled within the rock, coming to life under the glow of their headlamps.

Gil, the point man, stepped forward cautiously. He sought the concealed entrance to the subterranean cave system described by Abaddon. The chamber at the base of the rope ladder spanned about forty feet at its widest point.

Through the radio, Marty's voice crackled into existence. "Everything okay?"

Gil pressed the button on his walkie-talkie and responded, "Yeah, we're all here, no casualties. We're investigating what's down here."

Marty replied, "Roger that. Let me know if you need assistance."

Gil confirmed, "Will do."

In whispered tones, Arbuckle and Stretch engaged in a covert conversation. "He said no names," Arbuckle muttered, his voice barely audible. Stretch swiftly silenced his companion. "He said 'Roger.'"

Basic raised his voice, exasperation bubbling to the surface. "Will you shut that idiot up?"

Stretch intervened, muffling Arbuckle's protests with a gloved hand. " 'Roger' is just another way of saying 'okay,' so pipe down," he admonished. Arbuckle's childish response – tongue out – remained hidden beneath the veil of his headlamp's shadow.

Now, all four men gravitated toward the cavern walls. Basic attempted to dislodge a shimmering fragment embedded in the stone, but it stubbornly resisted his efforts. He shifted his focus to another piece nearby. Stretch nudged Arbuckle in a different direction, urging him to explore the cavern independently.

Gil, however, had found what he was searching for. The chamber's walls converged until he could touch both sides simultaneously. This narrowing corridor promised an entrance to the cave system hidden within the ravine, as described by Abaddon.

As Gil delved into his examination of the tunnel, an ominous sound disrupted his concentration. He spun around to find Basic pounding his boots against the ground while attempting to dislodge a shiny object. Each strike resonated with a deep bass tone, until the final blow produced a weak, splintering sound followed by a resounding crack.

Gil yelled at Basic, his warning arriving just half a second too late. "Basic, what are you standing on?"

Basic ceased his efforts and looked at Gil, then down at his own feet. "I don't know, but it sounds hollow." He stomped his foot, eliciting a resonant bass note. He stomped again, and this time, the sound was accompanied by the ominous sound of wood cracking.

Gil shouted desperately, "Get off that, Basic!"

Basic screamed as he plummeted into the chasm that had suddenly opened beneath him. The wooden platform he had been standing on, over four centuries old, had given way, despite its apparent thickness. Gil rushed to the edge, trying to save Basic, but it was too late.

Gil slid on his belly to the opening in the floor, peering into the dark void. Basic's headlamp was nowhere to be seen. Trembling, Gil retrieved his walkie-talkie and keyed the mic. "You there? Basic, you there?"

Marty's voice responded, "Who, me? Yeah, I'm here, kiddo."

Gil keyed the mic again, frustration and fear evident in his voice. "No, man. One of the guys went down a hole.

Basic, can you hear me?" His voice echoed in the chamber, resounding through the other two walkies.

There was no response. Gil scanned the depths of the hole with his headlamp, but it was too deep to discern anything.

He called down, "Basic, if you can hear me, say something." Silence was his only answer. Turning back to Stretch and Arbuckle, who stood close behind him, Gil instructed, "Stay clear of the edges, and watch your step."

Arbuckle quietly asked, "Where's Basic, boss?"

Gil shook his head. "I don't know, man. I don't know. God damn."

Reluctantly, Gil had to make the agonizing choice of moving on, leaving Basic's fate uncertain. Was this an unexpected trap? If so, avoiding it would be a straightforward task, as long as they understood what to look for. But something about the situation felt different, and Gil couldn't shake the nagging doubt that this wasn't a trap at all.

Gil, his senses sharpened by the accident, examined the wall where Basic had been rummaging. His actions were deliberate, measured. A subtle but determined stamp on the rocky floor reassured him – no hollowness, no hidden dangers. With meticulous care, he moved closer, extracting a lengthy piece of wood from the wall, its end adorned with a glistening obsidian arrowhead.

This was the source of the enticing sparkle that had drawn their attention. Obsidian, a volcanic glass coveted by select indigenous tribes, had been masterfully shaped into an arrowhead. Gil recalled museum displays showcasing obsidian's potential as a tool – primarily for knives. Much like glass, it dazzled under the caress of light. Now, it clung to the cavern walls like nature's hidden secrets.

With a single, deliberate motion, Gil tossed the arrowhead down the seemingly bottomless pit where Basic had vanished. An eerie silence prevailed as it fell. His companions, Arbuckle and Stretch, joined him, their faces obscured by the glow of headlamps and heavy hearts.

The mournful silence was only broken by Gil's succinct command, his voice carrying a weight of shared loss and foreboding, "Be careful." Both men nodded, their eyes averted, unable to meet each other's gaze.

Gil turned his focus toward the narrowing passage, a clear sign of their approach to the cave entrance. He took the lead, their headlamp beams cutting through the darkness. Silence held them tightly, their solidarity expressed in shared footsteps and vigilant watchfulness.

At last, Gil halted when the narrowing walls pressed against both shoulders, and he gazed upwards to a realization – they had already entered the cave. The rock overhead mirrored the stone embracing them from all sides. He turned to his comrades, his words measured, "We've found what we were looking for."

Arbuckle's fear broke the silence, "Can we go home now?" Stretch's swift reprimand, a friendly slap on the arm, silenced the outburst.

Gil, however, had other intentions. "Pretty quick," he said. "Let's take a moment or two to look around." Stepping back, he urged Arbuckle forward, his voice firm and unyielding, "You're the widest among us. Go as far as you can."

Arbuckle hesitated, eyes darting fearfully, until Gil's stern reminder spurred him to action, "What am I paying you for? Get in there, see how far you can go."

Stretch provided moral support, encouraging Arbuckle with a comforting pat on the shoulder. "You'll be fine, big guy. Gil just wants to test your limits. Watch your step, we've got your back."

Nervously, Arbuckle inched into the inky void, continually casting anxious glances back for reassurance. Stretch gestured onward, forcing Arbuckle to focus on his path. He had to twist his broad frame to squeeze through the narrowing crevice, his body brushing against unforgiving stone. Then, he suddenly stepped into a space that allowed him to face forward again.

With his back turned to Gil and Stretch, Arbuckle called back, his voice echoing ominously in the cavernous expanse, "Hey, it's real big over here." His words hung in the cavern, echoing with an unspoken fear that permeated their search.

Gil said, "Good man. Come on back, now Arbuckle."

"There's a funny looking thing," Arbuckle stepped farther into the darkness, "It looks like a bridge."

Gil was conflicted. He wanted Arbuckle to come back, but he was also curious about what was so interesting to the big man. Gil and Stretch exchanged looks and then ducked into the next chamber.

Arbuckle's discovery was a peculiar, log bridge. Gil couldn't resist investigating, even though he suspected a trap. He urged Stretch and Arbuckle to watch their step and moved closer to the log bridge.

Beneath his headlamp's pale glow, with a small jack-knife Gil excised a wood chip with the precision of a surgeon. Delicately, he raised it to his nose, inhaled the scent of the timber, and finally, he dared to touch it to his tongue. Recognition coursed through his senses like a long-forgotten memory. "It's hickory," he pronounced, "tastes just like my barbecue."

Gil rose from his crouched position and stepped toward the bridge. He extended his hand, and Arbuckle took it. Gil balanced precariously with one foot on each log. The logs wobbled beneath his weight, prompting him to spring back onto the safety of the outcropping. The far end of the logs responded with a mechanical grinding noise that reverberated through the cavern.

Crouching by the logs, Gil directed his light toward their connecting ends. Iron dowels anchored them to the rocks, causing the logs to pivot when pressure was applied. Gil attempted to turn one manually, but it resisted his efforts.

He nearly sliced a hole in his leather glove when his hand rubbed against a piece of obsidian that was embedded in the log. His headlamp revealed several more pieces of obsidian along the length of hickory.

 Undeterred, he transferred his weight onto one of the logs and noticed a subtle shift. Another turn, another ratchet-like noise from the distant side. "Shine your lights across the way. See if we can tell what that sound is."

Stretch and Arbuckle aimed their beams while Gil resumed his experiment. As the log turned and the ratchet noise persisted Stretch observed, "Something on the wall over there moved when you stepped on the log." Stretch's words were confirmed by Arbuckle's nod, prompting Stretch to speculate, "Could be a door?"

Gil confidently recognized this as one of the traps Abaddon had warned them about. It seemed deceptively straightforward: spin the logs to open a door on the opposite side and then cross the bridge. "Stretch," Gil proposed, "you're the smallest. I need you to test these logs and find out what's on the other side."

A moment of silence hung in the air before Gil prodded, "What's the matter? Are you only good with Arby taking the plunge?"

Arbuckle said to his friend, "Hey man. I'll go."

"No, Arby, Gil's right." Stretch touched his friend's shoulder.

"Stretch, you're the best fit for this." As Gil spoke, Stretch removed his jacket and unburdened himself of any excess weight. Gil handed him a length of rope, which he started to knot, but Arbuckle intervened, demonstrating a secure bowline knot. Stretch, illuminated by his headlamp, gazed in disbelief as Arbuckle chuckled to himself, "Heh, heh, Boy Scouts."

Gil then passed the other end of the rope to Arbuckle, who secured it with another bowline around his own waist. "I've got you, Stretch," Arbuckle assured him, carefully taking up the slack.

With tentative steps, Stretch tested the first log, gingerly tapping its surface. It initially resisted rolling but revealed a peculiar inclination. Stretch informed Gil, "This log only seems to want to roll inward." Gil nodded, recognizing the pattern.

Stretch, precariously balanced, applied outward pressure on one log and advanced to the next. Again, the log exhibited a preference for rolling inward. The ratcheting noise ceased. Stretch took three cautious steps.

"Ratchet" sounded from the distant side, and the left log shifted incrementally. Stretch's foot slipped, but he regained his balance and glanced back at Gil and Arbuckle with a wry smile. "Piece of cake," he quipped as "ratchet" echoed through the cave.

Stretch's foot wedged briefly between the logs, and he struggled to regain his balance. The logs ceased their inward movement, and the ratcheting noise ceased. Stretch dislodged his foot. Arbuckle gripped the rope with white-knuckled intensity, the darkness amplifying the tension in the air. The spectators held their breath as Stretch teetered, arms flailing, then gradually regained his balance.

Regret gnawed at Gil for sending Stretch out onto the logs, but there was no turning back now. He maintained a calm tone to soothe Stretch's nerves. "Guys, focus your lights on the other side. That sound must be connected to something moving over there." The trio directed their headlamps toward the distant wall, revealing a previously concealed void in the stone. "Stretch, you're more than halfway across. Keep going."

Stretch acknowledged Gil's encouragement with a nod and continued to inch forward. The "ratchet" sound interrupted his progress. His left foot brushed against an embedded piece of obsidian glass, momentarily throwing him off balance. The ensuing imbalance triggered three rapid ratcheting sounds. Stretch froze in place.

Arbuckle inched closer to the precipice causing the rope to slacken. He whispered under his breath, "Though I walk through the valley of the shadow of death," repeatedly reciting the only fragment of the psalm that surfaced in his memory. His friend, Stretch, was perilously close to the opposite side of the chasm. Arbuckle, preoccupied with his friend's safety, allowed the rope to brush against one of the logs.

As Stretch continued to shuffle along the logs, each step incited another "ratchet" sound. The slackened rope came into contact with the point where the logs intersected and caught itself on an obsidian shard. At the next ratcheting sound, the logs seized the rope. Stretch's progress was thwarted by the sudden resistance around his waist, nearly causing him to tumble forward. "Ratchet." Now, the rope was fully ensnared by the logs. Stretch dropped to his knees, straddling both logs, agony etched across his face as shards of obsidian pierced his flesh, and he cried out in pain.

Gil noticed the rope was tangled in the logs at about the same time as Arbuckle did. Arbuckle began tugging on the rope which caused the logs to vibrate. The piercing cuts on Stretch's legs made the logs slick. Stretch's right leg slipped into their jaws. Several ratchets sounded and he screamed in terror and agony. The logs were feeding him between them like the gears of a demonically-possessed paper shredder. The glistening obsidian shards dug into the flesh of his legs and blood was spraying as if from a garden hose.

Before Gil could stop him, Arbuckle slipped out of the bowline knot and bolted down the logs to try to save his friend. Gil shouted, "Stop Arby." But it was too late.

Arbuckle tripped and fell twice on his way causing the logs to part then come back together. This resulted in Stretch being pulled further into them. Every time the logs moved Stretch screamed and the ratcheting sound continued. By the time Arbuckle got to his friend, Stretch was consumed by the logs up to his rib cage. One arm was now in between the logs. Blood was everywhere. Arbuckle sat down on the logs to stop from falling. Several pieces of obsidian pierced his legs and his blood mingled with Stretch's. Then Arbuckle fell between the logs and both men struggled against the inevitable. Their own body weight was dragging them down between the logs. The obsidian shards were shredding them like confetti. Blood colored the logs and that god-awful ratcheting noise was constant. The portal on the other side of the crevice was now wide open.

Stretch stopped screaming when his rib cage was consumed by the logs. His head lolled to one side, rocking aimlessly as Arbuckle struggled to free himself.

Arbuckle screamed for a long time. Gil fell to his knees, safe on the outcropping, far from the blood. He knelt there listening to Arbuckle scream. After a few minutes the big man's screaming was reduced to intermittent moans. Then silence. The men's headlamp beams shone up to the ceiling.

As a final insult, there was a sudden flurry of ratcheting noises as the logs spun inward and their bodies fell through and tumbled down into the darkness. Gil watched their headlamp beams spiral down, get smaller and then disappear. He stood up and retreated the way they had come, back into the main chamber below the crypt.

Gil grabbed his walkie-talkie out of his pocket and keyed the mic. "Hey."

"Who me?" came from above.

"Yeah. I'm coming back up," Gil released the mic. Then continued, "Alone."

"Alone?"

"Yeah. We're gonna need some more guys." Gil started the long climb back up the rope ladder.

Marty replied, "Shit"

Yeah, thought Gil. Shit.

# THE SECOND SHIFT

Marty opened the door to Gil's apartment and ushered in the three new recruits, a noticeably younger and more refined trio compared to the initial batch he had introduced. As Gil contemplated the origin and background of these newcomers, he couldn't help but wonder how Marty had unearthed them. They assembled in the living room, facing Gil, who was seated at the kitchen table.

Once the apartment door was shut, Marty took center stage before the newcomers. "This is..."

Gil interrupted him with a raised hand. "Sorry, Marty. I don't want to know their names." He then stood and pointed at them, left to right, declaring, "You're Number One," jabbing his finger, "Number Two," and another jab, "And Number Three. Remember your numbers, and we'll be fine."

Marty apologetically shrugged at the three men. "Alright, you've got your numbers." He turned to Gil. "Is it okay to tell them your name, kiddo?"

Gil settled back at the table, took a sip of his beer, and nodded.

Marty addressed the assembled men, "This is Gil. He's the real number one around here. I told you pretty much all you need to know over the phone. Any questions?"

Number Three raised a hand, and Gil gestured for him to speak. "Where can I get changed? You said we're going underground? I don't want to get my good stuff dirty," he said, holding up a satchel as proof.

Gil pointed down the hallway behind Number Three. "Washroom is on the left. Change in there. We're leaving in five minutes. Don't dawdle."

The other two men equipped themselves with climbing gear, headlamps, work boots, and leather gloves. However, Number Three had already prepared himself, wearing his own work boots and gloves. Gil was impressed by the young man's work ethic, thinking he might make a valuable apprentice for future endeavors, provided they survived this job. That is, if there truly was an eighty-million-dollar prize hidden at the bottom of that cave. Then all bets were off.

The night before, Gil and Marty had loaded extra tools and supplies into a truck and transported them to the crypt. They made a quick stop at a local hardware store for two powerful flashlights, each boasting twelve-hundred lumens.

They loaded the three new recruits into the back of the truck and set out to continue their work. The ride was noticeably quieter than the previous day – silence enveloped them all. Gil remained lost in thought, wondering why everyone else was so quiet. Perhaps Marty had warned them.

The new recruits, on the other hand, accepted their task with a matter-of-fact attitude. Gil wasn't privy to the details of Marty's phone conversation with them, but judging from their demeanor, they weren't surprised by the crypt, the tunnel, or the rope ladder. Number Three, in particular, displayed a keen eagerness to descend to the depths below.

"First things first," Gil advised. They needed to lower the extra equipment by rope, including planks and a tool chest, as well as additional coils of rope and the new flashlights. They were nearly ready to begin.

"Hey, Number Three," Gil called out.

"Yes, sir?"

"You can descend now, and we'll lower water and some food down. Make sure no vermin or any unwanted guests get to it," Gil instructed, motioning toward a particular spot.

The young man, wasting no time, backed toward the rope ladder before Gil had finished speaking. Gil felt his anticipation building for the day's discoveries. Maybe it wouldn't be as daunting as he had initially feared. The loss of Basic, Stretch, and Arbuckle the previous day had left a bitter taste in his mouth, but Number Three's enthusiasm was infectious. It lifted Gil's spirits, and he shared a knowing smile with Marty. It was a bittersweet smile, but a smile nonetheless. They lowered the provisions without any issues, and Number Three confirmed by walkie, that all was well below.

Gil led the way for Numbers One and Two, ensuring there was a twenty-second gap between each climber to avoid a repeat of yesterday's incident with his hand getting stepped on. The descent was smoother today, as much of the effort to secure their footholds had already been done the day before. He also added a pair of latex gloves beneath his leather ones, although it didn't prevent his hands from sweating, but it did make him feel cleaner.

At the bottom, he found that Number Three had arranged the planks closer to the entrance of the outcropping, with the tool chest against one of the chamber's walls. The food and water were placed on top of the chest. Gil realized he needed to caution all three men about the possibility of rotting wood along the walls.

With everyone assembled, Gil showed them the spot where Basic had fallen, and then guided them to the limited space on the outcropping leading to the bridge. It was cramped with all four of them, and there was a risk of someone being accidentally pushed over the edge. Gil led them back out and explained their plan.

"We need to stabilize those two logs that will take us to the other side. They only turn in one direction, but we have to make sure they don't turn at all. So, we're going to nail some planks across them, essentially building a ladder across the ladder. Got it?" All three men nodded in agreement.

Number Three grabbed two planks and made his way back to the outcropping. He returned for another pair. Gil noticed the other two men leaning against the wall, engaged in casual conversation. An irritated Gil exclaimed, "What the fuck?" he yelled. "You can help or you can get the hell out of here." Numbers One and Two sprang into action, collecting the remaining planks and delivering them to the outcropping.

Meanwhile, Number Three came back and inquired about the best location for the food supplies. Gil guided him to the area where Basic had fallen through the floor. "Right about here should be fine. Watch your step. I don't think any rats will be coming near this spot."

Number Three grabbed a sack of twenty-penny nails and a claw hammer from the tool chest and disappeared into the narrow access leading to the outcropping. Gil was left alone in the chamber at the bottom of the rope ladder, listening to the distant sounds of hammering.

Marty's voice crackled over the radio, "Everything okay down there?"

Gil replied, "So far, so good. That Number Three kid is pretty enthusiastic, I have to say. Where'd you find him?"

"You really want me to say on the radio?"

Gil chuckled into the mic, "No, you're right. I forgot. Tell me later. I hear them hammering. I'll call you when we're across."

"Roger that, kiddo," Marty responded.

A pang of sadness washed over Gil as he recalled how Arbuckle had thought Marty was using someone's name when he said "Roger." Gil entered the narrow crevice that led to the outcropping, finding Number One standing on the edge, holding a plank for Number Two to grab. Number Three was already halfway across the log bridge, hammering a nail through a plank into the left log. Gil inspected their work so far.

The planks were nailed diagonally across both logs, providing a wider path when crossing the bridge. Gil watched Number Three as he used his hammer to break the obsidian glass embedded in the wood, making room for the next plank. When he reached the spot where Arbuckle and Stretch had fallen, he paused. Number Three knelt down and wiped the bloody stains with his gloved hand. He peered over the side, staring into the abyss. Shaking his head, he placed the next plank and hammered in another nail.

In less than half an hour, Number Three and his assistants, as Gil now considered the trio, had finished constructing the new bridge. Number Three stood on the other side, waving his hammer in the air. Numbers One and Two returned to the outcropping with Gil. "Good job," Gil commended them.

To Three, who was on the opposite side, Gil waved and called out, "Come on back." But Number Three waved his arms frantically, signaling "No." He pointed toward the dark opening behind him, eager to venture further into the cave system.

Gil was having none of it. "Come back now," he ordered. Though clearly disappointed, the young man obeyed. The bridge was now so stable that there were no unsettling creaks or wobbles and no ratchets. The gate on the other side was wide open.

Gil led the way for Number Three into the ante-chamber. He gathered all three men in a huddle. "Grab some water, have a bite to eat, and smoke if you need to. We're going to start exploring the other side in a few minutes. I want to warn you, it's not going to be safe. So, watch your step. If you see something, alert everyone. Got it?" All three of the young men nodded.

Water bottles were distributed, and sandwiches shared. Numbers One and Two sat quietly while they ate, while Number Three took the opportunity to initiate a private conversation with Gil. They moved away from the others.

"So, what are we doing down here, anyway?" Three asked, his curiosity piqued.

Gil chuckled at the thought of sharing the whole story with this young man. "Not today. But I have to say, I like your work ethic. You've got a good attitude. Keep it up, and when we're done here, I could use someone like you."

"Yeah? I'm not used to steady work, but okay. We can talk about it."

Gil continued, "Cool, Number Three. I'll get your name and details from Marty, and we'll work together. You're smart, and even better than that, you're clever."

Three asked, "What's the difference?"

"Clever means you know how to use smart," Gil explained, taking another bite of his sandwich. He stood and announced to the crew, "Alright, let's get this show on the road." Stepping to the spot where Basic had fallen, he indicated the hole, "You can toss your trash or empties down here." Numbers One and Two discarded their wrappers and empty bottles into the pit.

One lingered for a moment, watching the garbage disappear into the depths. "Looks deep," he observed.

Gil raised an eyebrow, "Yeah, we lost a guy down there on day one."

One said, "Shit. I'll bet that hurt."

Gil replied, "Let's not find out. Come on."

Leading the men into the crevice, where the ravine narrowed, Gil's thoughts centered on the bridge modifications. "Looks good," he muttered to himself. Stepping onto the bridge, he tested its stability with caution, his eyes on the planks, the logs, and the dark void below. The ironwood-hickory bridge proved itself sturdy, and Gil signaled his approval with a thumbs-up. "Good job, guys. I'll get across, and then you guys come after me, one at a time. Let's not push our luck." The three men nodded in agreement.

Gil proceeded cautiously, keeping his gaze fixed ahead, avoiding the mesmerizing blackness that lurked on either side. But fate had other plans. A misstep sent him tumbling, and his heart raced as he landed on his hands and knees perilously close to tumbling over the edge.

Behind him, the trio gasped in collective fear, but Number Three made a bold attempt to help. Gil sensed the vibrations of Three's approach before he heard it and swiftly yelled, "Stop!"

Three halted, and Gil, now on his feet, took a moment to regain his composure. As perspiration trickled down his face, he chuckled, thinking of the old adage, "Never let them see you sweat." In the pitch darkness, that seemed comically ironic. Laughter mixed with the lingering fear of a near-death plunge.

Gil addressed the men with newfound confidence. "I'm good," he assured them, and his would-be rescuer retreated to a respectful distance. "Thanks for jumping on, but I'm good."

Continuing his journey, Gil's headlamp revealed a stone border with an engraved inscription above the cave's entrance: VADE RETRO SATANA. Memories of his meeting with Abaddon resurfaced, and he muttered, "For fuck's sake. Is that, Latin?"

He wrote out the inscription in his note pad, capturing it for later scrutiny. Gil shifted his attention back to the bridge, the three men on the other side. The journey deeper into the cave beckoned, and he felt a strange sense of optimism about the day ahead. He waved the men to join him. Naturally, Number Three led the way. The other two waited until he successfully crossed, before risking the journey themselves.

Number Three, now on the same side, exhibited a natural curiosity and a sense of camaraderie. "You don't happen to read Latin, do you?" Gil inquired.

Three aimed his headlamp at the inscription, reading it aloud, "Vade Retro Satana?" He pondered for a moment. "I don't know, but I'd imagine Satana is either a Mexican guitarist or the Devil, like, you know, Satan."

Gil nodded in agreement. "That was my first thought, too. But the guitarist's name is Carlos, not Vade Retro." They shared a brief laugh. "So, probably the Devil, then." His memory flashed to his sarcastic laughter back in Abaddon's library. "Wonder what the first part says. I'll have to look it up when we get back topside."

From behind them, on the other end of the bridge, Number One activated the blinding high-lumen flashlight, casting an eerie glow upon the ancient stone wall confronting Gil and Three. The words had been meticulously etched into the rock face and it came into sharp focus. Turning toward his companions, he shielded his eyes against the harsh glare and signaled for Number One and Number Two to join them on their side of the rickety bridge. The aged span quivered and groaned under the weight of the two men hastening to their position, leaving the haunting darkness replaced by the blinding brilliance of the high-lumen light.

Gil explored the edge of the carved rock border which surrounded the recess. From the opposite end of the bridge, when the first two men were crushed between the logs, a gate barring the recess was raised, as the logs turned. That had been the source of the ratcheting noise. A hidden mechanism pulled the mysterious gate into the rock like a pocket-door you could find in a modern home. The fifteenth century was a pretty impressive era, if this was any indication.

With all four men gathered on the same side, Gil motioned for Number One to lead the way. The radiant cone of the flashlight, which had initially illuminated a fifty-foot expanse of rock, now dwindled to a mere pinprick as Number One guided them deeper into the caverns. Gil followed closely behind, with Three and

Two bringing up the rear, enveloped in the fun-house blackness of the cave.

The entrance to the underground cavern was a meandering tunnel, its smooth walls guiding them downward in a gentle descent. The men trod cautiously – their footsteps silent in the wake of the brilliant flashlight beam. A hushed stillness hung over them during their initial steps, allowing Gil's curiosity to awaken.

Slowing his pace to walk alongside Number Two, Gil inquired, "Did you notice any inscriptions on the rocks, or carvings of any kind?"

Number Two said, "Oh yeah. It was crazy. We were eating lunch, you know, and then I saw all these scratches." Then Two fell silent and continued walking.

Gil said, "And? What did you see?"

"Oh, sorry dude. I thought you already saw it. There are arrows in the walls."

"Yeah, we saw the arrow heads. You're talking about the arrow heads, right? Those shiny black glassy things?"

Two considered it for a second, "Nah, bro. I'm talking about a bunch of arrows carved into the rocks around the whole chamber. And they're all pointing down. There's like twenty of them, all around the whole space. I'll show you on the way out. Man, I thought you must have seen them. But like I said, I wouldn't have even noticed them if you hadn't, like, stopped for lunch. I thought they were natural, you know, like normal rock things. But then I noticed they were too well defined. And then there were a lot of them. Like, kind of freaked me out a bit. What do you think it means?"

Gil contemplated in silence for a moment. "No idea. All pointing downward, you say?" He continued, oblivious to Number Two's nod of agreement in the darkness. "Did you come across anything resembling words?"

"Oh, yeah," Number Two confirmed, "Just before the tunnel narrowed, I saw some writing. Wasn't a word I heard before. It looked like 'D-O-L-O-R,' but it wasn't a whole word, I don't think. Does that sound right, bro?"

Gil made another note in his book, "I wasn't even looking for things like that. Alright, good eyes, Two. We'll take a look on our way out." Gil grabbed the man's shoulder in appreciation.

They continued for another dozen yards before Number One halted abruptly, causing the team to bunch together within the confined tunnel. The stifling closeness of the space did nothing to ease Gil's claustrophobia, and he swallowed his rising anxiety.

The high-lumen flashlight projected its cone of light onto the wall ahead, revealing a chamber of approximately fifteen feet in height and twenty feet in width. This section of the cave exhibited meticulous hand-carved walls, a testament to the countless hours expended in its creation. Gil ventured closer, casting a diminishing shadow as he moved away from the light source, and began to discern finer details.

It became evident that they had unwittingly stumbled upon another trap. Within the circular recess, approximately two feet deep, rested a door, adorned with an inscription: "DISCINDO." Gil retrieved his notebook to record the inscription and called back to his companions, "Anyone here know what 'Discindo' means?" Silence prevailed, of course.

Stepping into the recess, Gil ran his fingers along the cold stone wall inside the circle. The craftsmanship was astounding; these carvings were the work of skilled artisans from four centuries ago, a testament to the dedication of those who had accompanied Fernando on his journey. Or of a more diabolical artisan, if he let himself think that way.

Within the recess, a door was constructed from the same wood as the bridge, but it bore a peculiar coating, similar to creosote. When Gil touched it, the wood felt slick. Two iron rings were bolted into the door, just below the top, and they didn't appear to be purely decorative. Wary of triggering any unknown mechanisms, Gil inspected the door, refraining from pushing or pulling until he comprehended the situation.

The door was solid and impeccably preserved. Two thick iron bands held it together. With no visible gap between the door and the rock wall, Gil noticed a fist-sized hole on the right side, perfectly aligned between the horizontal bands. He aimed his headlamp into the hole, but it only served to emphasize the darkness within.

Gil traced the edge of the hole with his finger tips. The wood felt smooth. He reluctantly slid his hand further into the hole a couple of inches. He prepared himself for jumping back in case something amiss took place.

He spun his hand around the opening, feeling it from top to bottom. About four inches into the hole, he felt another opening that went down at a ninety-degree angle. His fingers glided over the surface of something that felt like a handle. Gil withdrew his hand.

He shone his headlamp all around the door and the recess, again. There were six grooves, three to a side, etched into the stone. He made mental notes of what he'd observed. No visible hinges, zero clearance between wood and stone, preserved ironwood, two rings, two bands, one hole, grooves. There was not a lot to go on. He returned to the three men awaiting his directions.

"One, Two, I want you guys to open that door. There's a handle in that hole. I'm pretty sure that's what it is. Grip the handle, then we see what happens." Gil's voice demanded attention in the small space of the chamber.

Two took a step toward the doorway. One put his hand on Two's shoulder to stop him. Then One asked, "Is it safe?"

"Fucked if I know." Gil responded. "But this is what I'm paying you for, so get your asses moving."

One pointed at Three, "What about him?"

Gil stepped up to One and their noses almost touched when he said, "Does this guy have to do everything? What have you done to earn a dollar?"

Number Three stepped forward to intervene, "I can do it, Gil" Gil put his hand on Three's chest without taking his eyes off Number One.

Gil said, "No need, Three. Because One and Two are going to do it. Aren't you?"

Two shrugged angrily to dislodge One's hand from his shoulder and walked toward the recessed door. "Come on, man. Like don't fuck this up for us, dude." Two made his way to the doorway.

One waited a count of three and then nodded and blinked at Gil. He smiled and turned on his heel toward to the door.

One gave Two a subtle nudge, urging him to the outside, as he reached out with his left hand to probe the hollow cavity within the timeworn wood. His arm slipped into the recess up to his elbow, and a faint wince contorted his features, a testament to the physical demand of his efforts. Yet, the ensuing grin that crept across One's countenance, accompanied by a triumphant grunt, signaled a breakthrough, and he nodded at his partner in silent affirmation. A hollow clunk resonated throughout the chamber.

In response to their efforts, a sinister half-moon gap emerged, separating the door from its ancient frame. The two iron rings, flush against the door's surface at its peak, now hung at an angle. The door itself, a pivot upon a spindle that had penetrated the wood closer to its top than its midpoint, assumed an awkward slant, as if uneager to reveal its secrets.

Number Two seized both iron rings, perched high upon the door's facade, and exerted a downward force. The dark chasm at the door's base expanded, creating a rift between the ancient wood and the stone masonry. Gravity reclaimed the door with another decisive clunk, and Number One, frustration coloring his voice, erupted, "Dammit, man! Pull on that fucking thing!"

One's fingers plunged once more into the recess, their practiced movement triggering the anticipated clunk. The inky veil reappeared at the door's base. Number Two, throwing his weight into it, bore down upon the iron rings. The door's base creaked and swung open, surrendering to the man's persistence and granting them passage into the darkness beyond.

"I'm stuck."

One fell to his knees and his wedged arm pulled him into the space created by the swinging door. There was another audible 'crack', much louder than before, but this one sounded organic. One's arm snapped in the middle, breaking both his ulna and radius, midway between the wrist and elbow. His blood-curdling scream echoed into the darkness beyond the doorway.

Two tried desperately to swing the door back into its upright position, with no success. Having put his full weight onto the rings, it was now in a locked position, with the door perpendicular to the floor. There was a locking mechanism holding the door in place.

As One's agonizing cries reverberated through the cavernous depths, Gil and Three immediately sprinted toward the two figures. Chaos erupted in a whirlwind of events. Number Two, his weight bearing down on the ancient, rusted rings, had inadvertently swung the door into a secured position. Simultaneously, he unwittingly triggered a hidden stone treadle embedded in the floor. With a horrifying crack, Number One's arm snapped, eliciting a guttural scream that filled the chamber. And then, like something out of a nightmare, six razor-sharp blades sprang forth from the walls, cleaving both One and Two into three gruesome pieces. Their screams were silenced as quickly as they began, and the murderous blades nestled back into their concealed niches within the stonework.

Three and Gil froze in their tracks, transfixed by the hideous display. Blood flowed freely, creating a nightmarish tableau on the chamber floor. Gil's boots shone where the combined viscera splashed him.

In the aftermath, a dim, mechanical ticking emanated from within the cave's walls, a disconcerting reminder of the sinister intricacies hidden within the depths. One's and Two's dismembered remains collapsed into a grotesque mound at the very threshold of the deadly door.

"Jesus," Three muttered, his voice barely rising above a whisper.

Gil, still grappling with the shock of the unfolding horror, struggled to find words.

Three took a step forward and Gil touched the man's elbow. He just shook his head. "Don't."

"This is your fault," Three's accusation hanging heavy in the stifling air.

"Yep," Gil admitted, his tone devoid of remorse.

"That could have been me?" Three's voice trembled with a mix of fear and anger.

"Yeah, or me."

A trace of cold detachment in Gil's voice sent shivers down Three's spine. "You don't seem very upset about this."

Gil snorted wryly, his eyes scanning the chamber with a calculating gaze. "No, I'm not. I expected something. Not exactly like this, but something. There are traps all throughout this place." He took a deliberate step forward. "Stay here."

Gil approached the doorway. His boots sloshed through the pooled blood. It was already beginning to congeal. Strands of clots stuck to his feet as he strode through the mire.

The blades that cut through the two men, had retreated into the notches in the stonework. They dripped blood and entrails. The stench of shit rose from the heap of flesh. Gil called out, "Three?"

Three intimated, "I think you should start calling me Jimmy."

Gil nodded.

Jimmy asked, "What do you need?"

"Jimmy, we're going to need a dolly and something to pack these guys into. Run back to the base of the ladder and walkie Marty to drop a couple of those big plastic buckets down the hole. Maybe more than a couple."

Jimmy turned and headed back toward the main chamber.

"Oh, and Jimmy, maybe a pitchfork? I don't know, a shovel at least."

That gave Jimmy pause. Without looking at Gil, he nodded and ran across the bridge and disappeared.

Gil turned to the gruesome task at hand. He grabbed the top slice, which was Two's chest and shoulders, and pulled that out and tossed it behind him. It splashed and Gil got some on his face. "Nice. Real fucking nice."

Sorting through alternating pieces of One and Two, Gil cleared a few of the body parts from out of the doorway. Gil heard a low, distant rumble as Jimmy maneuvered a dolly across the bridge.

It echoed through the darkness, the noise akin to a drum duel, heralding Jimmy's entrance into this subterranean slaughterhouse. Huge empty plastic buckets were the source of the racket.

Jimmy immediately grasped the situation, tossing remnant pieces of "One" and "Two" into the gaping mouths of the buckets. It wasn't rocket-science by any stretch of the imagination. And there was no easy way to perform this job. By the time he was finished Jimmy had transformed into a Jackson Pollock forgery composed of gore and ooze.

Gil, had to laugh. "Jimmy, you know there's no showers down here, right."

Jimmy took account of himself. He realized he must look a sight and smiled at himself. He flicked large dollops of viscous blood off his fingertips. He said, "You should talk. You look like you've been eating spaghetti in an earthquake."

That broke whatever tension there was and both men began laughing right out loud, revelling in their graveyard humor. Gil sat down hard onto something soft. When he turned, he saw that he was sitting on what was left of One's ass. That made him laugh even louder.

One's wallet was in his back pocket. Gil retrieved it. He read the driver's license. "Says here his name was Archie."

Jimmy chuckled, "Like in the comic books? Like comic-book Archie?"

"Yeah. Fucking Archie. Says here, Height, six feet, one inch."

In unison, Gil and Jimmy yelled, "Not anymore."

Jimmy laughed so hard at that, that he, too, had to sit down. Both men were slapping their knees and rocking back and forth on their butts. They kept at it for another full minute. Gil wiped tears from his eyes with a bloody hand, and that made him laugh a bit longer.

Jimmy stopped laughing first. He looked sad. He hung his head and looked at his hands, and then at his feet. "What are we doing here, Gil?"

Gil chuckled a little and took a deep breath and let it out in a long, deep sigh. He raised his head and stared at Jimmy. "Eighty-million reasons," was all he said.

That caught Jimmy's attention. "Eighty-million what?"

"Dollars."

"Dollars?"

"Dollars."

"Where?"

Gil aimed his thumb into the darkness beyond the doorway. "In there, and maybe down a hundred feet. Maybe."

"Maybe?"

"Yeah, maybe. I didn't believe the guy who told me about it, but now, this is the second trap, so. Definitely, maybe."

"Definitely maybe? And you're risking lives on a maybe?"

"Sure. Not risking MY life. But, yeah, sure. I'll sacrifice a few lives. Eighty-million. Why not?"

Jimmy's face hardened. He stared at Gil. "That's pretty cold."

Gil shrugged off the insult. He said, "Let's get back to work. Help me with these two assholes." Gil patted Archie's bloody buttocks.

The joke registered. Jimmy didn't laugh, but he stepped forward and together he and Gil packed the leg pieces into two buckets. They positioned the buckets on the dolly and manhandled the awkward load across the bridge into the main chamber.

Jimmy asked, "Are we going to take these up and dispose of them?"

"Nope." Gil maneuvered the dolly to the hole Basic had dropped into on their first day.

Jimmy objected, "Nah, come on man. We can't do that? No burial? I don't know."

Gil had enough. He let go the dolly and grabbed Jimmy by the throat, with his left hand. He pushed the smaller man backwards up against the wall. One of the obsidian arrow heads caught his eye in the light beam off his headlamp. He reached for it with his right hand and plucked it from the wall and held it to Jimmy's throat, all in one deft movement.

Gil said, "Do you know why you're not dead, right now?"

Jimmy struggled to shake his head.

"Because I need you. Do you want to continue to be needed, or discarded? Because you can be discarded and replaced as easily as we're going to replace Tweedle-One and Tweedle-Two, here. Do you understand?"

Jimmy nodded. Gil let go of his throat and then he tossed the arrowhead down the hole. It clicked and clacked as it bounced off the sides of the hole and then it was gone.

Gil slapped Jimmy softly on the side of the face with the palm of his bloody-gloved hand. "Relax. I like you."

"Got a peculiar way of showing it," Jimmy retorted.

Gil let out a low, smoky laugh. "Let me confer with Marty, see about getting you a slice of the pie."

Jimmy's laughter mirrored Gil's. "A slice of what? A maybe? What's thirty percent of zilch?"

Gil's laugh turned to a wry grin. "It won't be thirty, that's for fucking sure. It's a definite maybe, so hold your horses. But I'll have to chat with Marty. He and I are equals, you're an afterthought."

Gil returned to his side of the dolly, the weighty buckets in tow. He upended one of them, and the crimson contents slithered out into the abyss, creating a gruesome symphony of wet thuds as the contents bounced off the walls. Gil tossed the empty bucket into the void, an act of nonchalance that contrasted with the sinister choreography.

His eyes locked onto Jimmy, then the remaining bucket on Jimmy's side of the dolly. It was a pivotal moment. If Jimmy complied with dropping the bodies, then he was in. If not, then Jimmy might be going down the hole next.

Jimmy's face wrestled with the turmoil raging in his soul. After an agonizing moment, he leaned in, scooped up one of the buckets, and flung its gory contents into the pit. Gil sensed an almost inaudible apology in the air. He didn't care if Jimmy's cooperation was grudging; he demanded obedience above all else.

With the last fragments of the viscera sent plummeting into darkness, Jimmy tossed the buckets in as well. Gil beckoned him closer. Together they returned to the wooden door.

Gil sidestepped the growing pool of blood, his boots and clothes tarnished in a grotesque tapestry. At the doorway, Gil examined the blades that sliced through the two men. They were made of steel and they were pitted with rust, but they were thick enough to withstand four centuries of oxidation. Gil ran his finger along the business edge of the blade. It was still sharp enough to leave a small slice in his leather glove. The blades criss-crossed each other as if they were three pairs of scissors that had over-extended themselves. The notches in the stone in which the blades now rested, were chiselled with something larger and stronger than these blades.

Gil examined the wooden door. The iron rings hung vertically from the now-horizontal door. Gil grasped one of the rings and pulled on it. There was still some give in the swing of the door. The nearest edge, the top of the door, dropped an inch with Gil's weight, but then it went back up when he relaxed. The door remained in a locked position. There was enough space between the flat door and the floor for a person to crawl through on hands and knees.

Just inside the stone niche that supported the wooden door, he saw a rectangular piece of stone that rocked back and forth when pressed upon. There was a fulcrum beneath the stone. He figured, rightly, that this was the triggering mechanism that activated the blades.

Gil leaned down and aimed his headlamp into the darkness beyond the opened wooden door. It appeared that there was a small room with an opening on the opposite wall from this one. That might be a stairwell, or a severe right-angled hallway. No way to tell from this vantage point.

Stepping back, he faced Jimmy. "Time to head topside and gear up for tomorrow. We've got two new faces to introduce to this place."

Jimmy nodded, contemplative. "We should bring down some water to clean this mess. I don't fancy crawling through this...shit. And if we're going to sacrifice more folks, it's better if they don't see it coming."

Impressed by Jimmy's pragmatism, Gil added, "Agreed. I'll leave that to you. And remember, don't breathe a word about the eighty million to anyone, anywhere."

Jimmy grinned, a silent promise hanging between them. "Partner."

Gil returned the sentiment, "A silent partner. Let's go."

It was slow climbing up the rope ladder, this time. Their blood-soaked gloves made for slippery grips on the rungs. And fatigue from stress and adrenalin made the climb that much more tedious. Gil was happy to let Marty drive the truck back to the motel. He and Jimmy stretched out in the back and felt every bounce and bump in the road.

Gil felt a twinge of guilt at the thought of stringing Jimmy along. The kid was clever and able and for now he was needed. If he followed orders as he has been doing, then he was going to survive another day. But there was no way the kid was getting a share. Too many bad things could happen in that cave system. Guaranteed.

## THE LADIES

"You want names this time, Gil?" Marty inquired as two women strode into the motel room, presenting an image of strength and determination.

Gil appraised the women. They both looked fit. They both had well defined biceps and quads. These were women that worked out, or worked hard at their jobs. And their attitudes said they were not to be messed with. "Yeah. We'll take names on these two." Gil gestured for the women to join him at the dining table, "Ladies."

Marty, ever the charismatic operative, broke the ice with his signature charm. "Gil, allow me to introduce Leah and Angelica, sibs from south of the border," he remarked, his mischievous grin implying a more intimate connection. "Sorry, not south of our border, south of the U.S. border. These women hail from Mexico."

There was an unspoken history between Marty and the two women, evident in his uncharacteristic behavior – he had never exhibited such a schoolboy infatuation. Turning to the women, Gil inquired, "Has Marty explained what we need?"

Angelica spoke for the pair, her tone displaying a mix of curiosity and confidence. "He says you're going on some Tomb Raider bullshit and need some muscle," she flexed her sculpted arms in a display of strength, a sense of humor in her voice. "Well, we're your muscle, darling," both women laughed. Marty joined in the merriment. They showcased their chiseled arms, expertly manipulating their muscles in a hypnotic performance that captivated Marty, though it left Gil unmoved. He shook his head in disbelief at Marty's reaction.

With a raised eyebrow and a disapproving sigh, Gil uttered, "Wonderful," he muttered dryly. He exchanged a glance with Marty, conveying his desire for seriousness. Marty promptly ceased his giddy laughter, and the room's atmosphere intensified.

Marty declared, "Ladies, let's grab some gear and get this show on the road,"

## THE BOTTOM OF THE WELL

Sixteen hours had passed since Marty led the women to the truck, and Gil drove everyone to the crypt.

In the darkened and empty motel room, a sudden and thunderous banging echoed through the air, shattering the silence. Gil's frantic voice cut through the noise of keys jangling and fists pounding at the door. "Goddamn thing. Can't see shit in this light."

The scratches of the key against the lock ended as it finally found its mark, and Gil flung open the door. Both he and Marty stumbled into the pitch-black apartment, their faces etched with dread. Marty collapsed into a large armchair, his trembling hands covering his face, and he began to sob uncontrollably.

Gil, disoriented and shaken, fell to the floor just inside the doorway. With a swift kick, he closed the door, a sound that reverberated like a gunshot, causing Marty to bolt upright in alarm. Realizing it was only the door, Marty sank back into the chair, his head resting against it, and he let out a desperate cry, "What the fuck was that?"

Gil's head rocked back and forth as he lay on the floor, moaning and then suddenly shouting, "Fuck! Fuck! Jesus Christ."

The visible distress on both men was undeniable. Gil curled into a fetal position on the floor for a minute. Then he stood and fumbled for the light switch, revealing the extent of the horror that had unfolded. Blood covered Marty from head to toe, saturating the chair's fabric. Gil, his own body similarly drenched in crimson, recognized the severity of the situation. I need to get rid of that chair, now. I liked that chair, he thought.

Marty raised his tear-streaked face and stared at his blood-soaked friend, his voice quivering with disbelief. "What happened down there? What the ever-loving fuck?"

Gil, having filled a kettle with water and set it on high, took a seat at the dining table, reflecting on their ordeal. He, too, was drenched in blood, his boots squishing as he moved. He wiped his face with his hand, flinging droplets onto the floor. "I don't know, Marty. I just don't know." His tone softened, and he asked, "Are you hurt?"

Marty and Gil examined themselves. Gil thought, this much blood and none of it mine? Marty's voice still trembling. "I don't think so. God, kiddo, so much blood. How?"

Gil sighed and continued, "Okay. Look." He closed his eyes and pictured the day, "We got the girls to the crypt. Jimmy was waiting for us there. Introductions were made. Me, the girls, and Jimmy descended into the hole. We had ropes, walkies, batteries, and water. Did we miss anything up top?"

Marty directed his gaze to the ceiling, his voice quivering, "I didn't see anything."

"We got them down to the first chamber," Gil explained. "Jimmy and I showed Leah and Angelica the work so far – the hole Basic went into, the bridge, and the door that killed One and Two. We didn't elaborate on who or how anyone died, but it was evident that something terrible had happened, with the blades still there and the stench of meat and shit hanging in the air.

We got to the opening I told you about. It led to a stairwell. The stairs lined the wall with a very wide empty space in the middle. I remember that freaked me out a little bit. I stepped out onto the first riser and looked down. It was just black on black. I took a light-stick and cracked it and tossed it in."

Marty lifted his head off the chair. "You did that? Not Jimmy?"

"Jimmy was eager to start the descent, but I made him wait. The women were more patient, and maybe he could sense a danger," Gil replied. "He was always keen, so maybe that was just his style." The shrieking kettle on the stove demanded their attention, startling both men.

Gil rushed to the stove to silence the kettle, then fetched two cups and tea bags. He handed a cup of tea to Marty. "Here. Chamomile, it's calming."

Marty accepted the tea with gratitude and took a sip. "I feel calmer already. Thanks, kiddo."

Gil snorted softly. "Yeah, me too." Gil took a deep breath. "So, these stairs went down along the wall in a wide spiral. There was this old rope tethered to the wall with iron hooks. I remember I backed off the step and asked one of the ladies to go get another coil of rope. She trotted back to the first chamber."

Gil stared up at the ceiling, lost in thought. "Hey. When she came back with the rope, you were with her. What was up with that? When did you come down? You've never done that before."

As they sipped their tea and tried to make sense of their gruesome experience, Marty, furrowing his brow, struggled to recall the details. "I don't remember coming down. I just remember being down. I must have climbed down." He closed his eyes and strained to remember. "I can see myself at the bottom of the ladder."

Gil took a moment to absorb this information. "Hm."

Marty commented, "Yeah, 'hm'."

Before Gil resumed the story, Marty marveled at their work so far. "That bridge work is pretty cool. You did that?"

"No, that was all Jimmy," Gil replied. "He was good with his hands, a natural."

They sipped their tea, collecting their thoughts.

Gil continued, "Jimmy grabbed the rope and started stringing it along the iron hooks. He got way ahead of everyone, almost running. I yelled at him to slow down, but he only did a little. Then he was off again. That was a really long coil of rope."

Marty contemplated this and asked, "Did I say something strange when we were down there?"

Gil recalled, "You said a word I couldn't understand, something like 'obtero.'"

Marty repeated the word to himself. "Obtero? You really think I said that? Obtero?"

"Any idea what it means?" Gil inquired.

"Not a clue," Marty responded.

Gil recalled the Latin inscriptions they encountered on the first day. "Hey, there was Latin written all over the place down there. Remember on that first day, the words over the doorway and on the walls? Carved into the rocks."

Marty leaped out of his chair, searching for something. "Yeah, you made me run out and buy a dictionary, an English to Latin one. I got it. Where did I put it?" Marty patted his pockets absentmindedly while he pondered. Then, as if struck by inspiration, he shouted, "Bedroom!" He dashed down the short hallway, sloshing and squishing with blood, and returned with a small red book, Cassell's New Latin Dictionary, its gold print glistening. "Found it!" he exclaimed, handing the book to Gil and awaiting his approval like an eager puppy.

Gil found "Obtero" in the Latin dictionary. The definition, after their recent experience, sent shivers down his spine. He mumbled, "To crush. To destroy. To break to pieces"

Marty's shock was palpable. "That's horrible," he muttered. It was an understatement.

Gil said, "Yeah. But why did you say it. You don't speak Latin."

Marty thought for a second. "I don't know. You're sure I said it?"

"Of course, I'm sure. Wait a minute. Did you see that word somewhere in the room we were in? Other words were carved into doorways and on the walls. I made notes. Hang on a sec." Gil rifled his pockets for his notebook. When he found it, it was soaked through with blood, just like everything else he wore. He peeled the pages open to the entries he made when they encountered the other words.

Gil looked up Discindo. He ignored Marty trying to peer over his shoulder. Gil spoke softly to himself as he read, "Discindo. Christ. To cut into pieces. Jesus." He dragged his fingers through a few more pages until he found Dolor. "Pain? What the fuck. Dolor means pain."

Gil closed the dictionary with a snap. "Jesus, Marty. These are warnings. Are you sure you didn't see obtero on the wall or something?"

"Maybe, kiddo. Sorry. I don't remember saying anything like that."

Gil said, "Yeah. But that one word explains a lot."

Marty put his hand on Gil's shoulder. "Not your fault, if you're blaming yourself."

Gil shouted at the older man, "How could this be my fault? I don't speak Latin."

Marty chuckled as he moved to the easy chair and sat down. "Well, you did kill Abaddon about two minutes before he was going to warn you about the traps. He may even have had information that would have saved us eight lives. So, maybe a little of this is on you."

"Fuck you, Marty. What happened today, I don't think could have been prevented even if we did know the definition of obtero. So, to hell with you."

"You don't believe in Hell."

"Of course not. What's that got to do with anything? No, I don't. And I'm starting to not believe in you either."

Marty laughed so hard a glob of clotted blood dislodged itself from his hair and tumbled down his face. "Well, now you're just trying to hurt my feelings."

"You have those? You'd be hard pressed to prove it."

"Me? You should talk. I remember our first job. That blood bank thing. I killed that woman you were about to rape." Marty shouted that last word, for effect. "You begged me not to make you an accessory to murder?" He pointed an accusatory finger at Gil. His hand shook with rage. "You changed your tune when you started making money, kiddo. It's always been about the money for you. And now, eight people are dead and for what? More money. You don't need more money. I don't need more money. Hell, I don't need any money. I'm done. A junkie's death for me, I don't care. It all started to wear on me. When we hit the bikers? I knew that was my last job. Then Abaddon made me recruit for him. That paid a few bills, got me high, got me laid once in a while. But I think it's affecting my brain. I have no idea what went down today. But I feel like we're responsible for all of it."

Gil mumbled, "Speak for yourself."

Marty scowled. "Okay. I feel responsible. I called all of them to come in on this. And it's ended so badly."

Gil jumped. "Ended? It's not fucking ended. We were at the bottom of the that thing. I mean how long did that priest…"

"Monk," Marty corrected.

"Friar. I think Fernando was a friar. Regardless. How long did he spend on these things? He had to get back to the east coast. He came to the west coast. He did all this. Then he headed back and got killed by the east coast natives. That has to be the bottom. That thing we saw has to be the last door."

Marty shook his head in disbelief, not disagreement. "So, what happened after I said that obtero thing?"

Gil thought about it. Then he said, "You said 'obtero' and the women looked at you. They're Spanish, but maybe they must have heard some Latin along the way.

Jimmy was already hauling ass down the stairs. He had rope strung along the wall in the hooks. I tied off this end of the rope and I joked, 'ladies first'. Leah and Angelica led the way. You went next and I took up the rear. Everybody's headlamps illuminated the passage down. It looked like a piece of cake.

The steps oozed with moisture – the surfaces dangerously slick. I offered silent gratitude for Jimmy's work. The rope was a lifeline."

From the depths, Jimmy's voice ascended like an echo. His headlamp flickered far below, barely visible. He urgently cried, "We need more rope!" Gil tried to remember if it was Leah or Angelica who he sent back to retrieve and then ordered down the steps to deliver the rope.

Marty chimed in, "It was Angelica, this time. I remember she darted past me, and I almost sent her tumbling into the open space. It scared the shit out of me."

"Right, Angelica. I recall you screaming like a baby when she nearly dropped off the edge. You caught her, Marty. That was a good save," Gil commended.

Marty nodded thoughtfully. "It felt like I saved her. Oh God, what is this place? I remember Abaddon kept saying that getting to the gold would require sacrifice. I always thought he meant hard work, not human beings."

Gil continued, "Angelica returned with more rope after only a couple of minutes. She hurried past us and descended the stairs to join Jimmy. Of the four of us trailing behind him, she was the only one who caught up. However, when he got the fresh rope, he left her behind to secure it. By the time we reached Angelica, she had fastened her end tight. Jimmy seemed to be in a hurry, practically sprinting down the staircase. I glanced upwards, and the world above us had vanished entirely."

Jimmy's cheers shattered the oppressive silence, announcing the discovery of the stairwell's end. Gil shouted a warning for him to watch for traps. He laughed, and that laughter was the last the five of them would hear underground. The men and women on the stairs lagged at least five minutes behind Jimmy. And the stairs were perpetually drenched.

"Did you, by any chance, think it was water too?" Marty inquired. "I thought that the entire way."

Marty's question prompted Gil to ponder. "I can't recall if I thought anything of it until we reached the bottom and saw it pooling in the corners. I couldn't figure out where it came from. That was an unimaginable amount of blood. If I didn't know better, I'd say the god-damned cave was bleeding."

Gil scratched his chin, taking a sip of now-cold tea. "Only in hindsight does it begin to make any sense."

Marty thought for a moment before responding, "Hindsight? As in, we never should have gone to Abaddon's place?"

Gil chuckled. "Maybe. But we'll have to see when we go back."

Marty expressed shock, "Back? You want to go back?"

Gil shouted in exasperation and threw his hands in the air, "Of course! There could be eighty million dollars in gold down there. After all we've suffered, I'm not ready to give up. If we've been fools, so be it. But if not, a king's ransom, split two ways — that's what I'm hoping for."

Marty mulled it over before replying, "For a man who thought Abaddon was a fake and a liar, you're surprisingly optimistic."

Gil chuckled. He replayed the scene in his mind and said, "So, Jimmy was hooting and hollering. We reached the bottom, where the stairs were still drenched. And, yeah, I thought it was water until then, too."

It was three in the morning, and exhaustion clung to their faces and voices like a shroud. They had departed at eight the morning before, accompanied by Jimmy, Leah, and Angelica. Yet, when the subject of the blood arose, it was as if a veil had been lifted, illuminating the room. They both sat up straighter, their eyes locked, and in unison, they exclaimed, "Jesus Christ."

Gil started, "All that blood. Maybe Abaddon wasn't full of shit after all. The first two traps were man-made, conquerable with logic and mechanics. But that blood... what in the hell was that?"

Marty concurred, "Hell may be the explanation."

Gil nodded, "Hell? Yeah. But Jimmy didn't wait for us at the bottom. We raced down through all that shitty muck, and when we reached the bottom, he was gone."

"Right," said Marty.

"I stepped off the stairs, and that's when I noticed it was all bloody. The four of us then tried to follow Jimmy's trail. But there were no tracks. The floor was submerged in a river of blood. We had no choice but to wade through it."

Marty interjected, "I remember that. We ventured into a tunnel at the bottom of the stairs, and the blood kept getting deeper. We had to swim through it."

Gil confirmed, "Yeah. Jimmy was nowhere in sight, and we got through all that blood. I called out his name, but there was no response. Then panic began to set in. I hoped he was safe, but I also couldn't shake the fear that he might somehow run off with the gold."

Marty agreed, "I had those same thoughts, both of them."

Gil continued, "Imagine contemplating that while wading through a river of blood. You know what else crossed my mind?"

"What?" Marty inquired.

"Abaddon. Remember when you said, 'I killed him two minutes too soon'? I wondered if he might have warned us about this."

Marty shrugged. "Too little, too late."

Gil went on, "As we got down the tunnel, I spotted a faint light reflecting off the walls, and I assumed it was Jimmy. And that's when parts of the ceiling collapsed on us."

"Wait, the ceiling collapsed on us?"

"Yeah, maybe that's why our memories are so foggy."

"That would make sense. I think I recall something hitting my head, and then everything went dark," Marty said, touching the back of his head and temples, searching for blood and finding a lot of it, but none of it his.

Gil scratched his chin and took a sip of his still-cold tea. "It was only a minor cave-in. I saw that faint light in the distance. You were right beside me, but looking back, you were acting kind of wonky."

"If you say so."

Gil confessed, "You know, until that moment, I had been convinced the Abaddon-Devil nonsense was bullshit. But what I saw, and maybe you saw it too, left me with serious doubts."

Marty, his posture defensive and alert, inquired, "What did you see?"

Gil hesitated, fearing that his account would sound ridiculous. "I saw Jimmy, his back to us, working on the lock on the next door. Standing behind him were Basic, Stretch, and Arbuckle. But that couldn't be, because they're all dead. And then, add to my confusion, One and Two — do you remember them? — moved to flank Basic and Arbuckle. All five of those dudes were standing there, behind Jimmy while he was working on that lock. And that's when it struck me."

Marty leaned in closer, hanging on every word, "Struck you with what?"

Gil closed the gap between their faces until they nearly touched, his voice a raspy whisper. "It dawned on me, like a lightning bolt, where I'd seen Jimmy before."

Marty slid to the edge of his seat.

Gil's voice dropped to an almost inaudible level as he divulged, "Jimmy was the cop I saw, stationed at Abaddon's house. I saw him stop the ambulance guys at the door. Now, I get it. He searched Abaddon's body before allowing them to take it away. The key's been in his possession all along. No wonder he was so eager to lead the way."

Marty's reaction was explosive; he tumbled from the easy chair, landing unceremoniously on the floor. "Fucks sake!"

## THE CRYPT

Gil and Marty led the women down the winding, dimly lit staircase that clung to the wall like an ancient secret passageway. Jimmy had raced ahead, his headlamp vanishing far into the inky blackness of a tunnel. The stairs now bore witness to a sinister transformation as liquid oozed from the walls. By the time they reached the foot of the stairs, the liquid had risen to their ankles, and a few steps further down the tunnel, it reached their shins.

Gil played the beam of his headlamp side-to-side, revealing the walls discharging a thick, red, viscous substance into the tunnel. It coursed along the floor, and when the liquid reached knee-deep, Gil's curiosity got the best of him. He dipped his fingers into the crimson flow and inspected it in the pale, artificial light. The distinctive scent of copper reached his nostrils, and a chilling realization dawned on him. "My God," he whispered, "this is blood."

Marty passed Gil, deeply unsettled by the sight of the tunnel's gruesome transformation. Leah and Angelica followed, their faces etched with dread, and there was still no sign of Jimmy. Gil, momentarily shaken by the bloody revelation, resumed his march.

Further ahead, Marty halted abruptly, his instincts on high alert. "Gil, do you feel that?"

Gil paused, his senses on edge, trying to discern what Marty had sensed. It didn't take long for it to manifest—a subtle but distinct draft, an intermittent breeze that first caressed their faces and then pulled at them from behind. Gil acknowledged, "Yeah, I feel that. There must be an exit down here. Have you seen anything of Jimmy?"

Gil made his way past the women to join Marty. "Can't see a damn thing ahead," Marty muttered.

A sudden gust of air assailed them, and in that very moment, a jagged chunk of rock plummeted from the tunnel's ceiling. Gil managed to evade the fist-sized piece, but Marty was less fortunate; it struck him on the side of his head and shoulder, causing him to tumble into the blood-filled stream. Gil and Leah lunged to his rescue. Their efforts prevented him from going under. Gil couldn't help but notice the gentle care Leah bestowed upon Marty. I'll have to ask Marty about their history when we get back, thought Gil. Then amended that thought to, if we get back.

The air grew foul as the blood continued to rise, now reaching their waists as they trudged further in pursuit of Jimmy. Around a bend in the passage, a faint glow from Jimmy's headlamp beckoned them. Gil called out Jimmy's name, but there was no response. They continued wading through the blood, with Leah supporting Marty and Angelica trailing behind.

Then the air took on an unbearable stench. Gil recoiled, and one of the women gagged. Through her fingers, Leah inquired, "What is that?"

Something peculiar was unfolding near Jimmy as he worked on the door lock. A dense, swirling cloud began to form, accompanied by a peculiar buzzing or humming. Jimmy turned to investigate the disturbance, and the light from his headlamp cast his face in an eerie new light, revealing a detail Gil hadn't noticed before.

Suddenly, it all fell into place. Gil's memory took him back to the night he killed Abaddon and rifled through the dead man's pockets. There, at the doorway to Abaddon's mansion, stood Jimmy, the police officer who had stopped the ambulance drivers. That's why Gil found nothing. And it explained Jimmy's urgency to reach this place.

Gil asked Leah, "Did you bring any weapons?"

Leah replied, "Angelica has baseball bats in that sack she's carrying. I think she also has a machete."

"Good," Gil said, his tone grim. "Get them out and be prepared for anything." Leah tapped Angelica on the shoulder, and the two women armed themselves as best they could.

Up ahead, the undulating cloud fractured into several fragments. The hum grew louder, and the darkened shapes emitted a pungent odor that clawed at their senses. Gil fought to breathe, and the shapes materialized into human forms. Jimmy's piercing scream filled the tunnel as he found himself surrounded by five eerie figures. Jimmy's headlamp rendered the figures as menacing silhouettes from Gil's perspective, but as one of them turned, Gil's jaw dropped in disbelief. It was Basic. But Basic was dead.

The other figures, Stretch and Arbuckle, were no less unsettling. They appeared even more grotesque, as if they had been torn apart and haphazardly sewn together. The mere sight of it defied all reason, with fingers growing from strange places and limbs in the wrong positions. It was all wrong.

The chamber was cloaked in an eerie stillness, a sinister tableau painted with grotesque figures and frenzied chaos.

Basic, his body a patchwork of mutilation, stood at the center of the stage, an embodiment of suffering. His injuries were a testament to the horrors that surrounded him. No emotion flickered on his wounded face, a mask concealing torment and pain beneath.

Stretch and Arbuckle flanked Basic, their bodies shattered beyond recognition, like fragments of a puzzle pieced together without regard for human anatomy. Their grotesque distortions left a sickening impression, as if a lunatic attempted to recreate the human body without instructions.

To Basic's left, the two victims of the ancient blades had been hastily reconstructed. They bore the disfigurements of hurried patchwork. It was as though a frenzied doctor had attempted to put them back together with complete abandon. Number One's pitiable attempts to communicate, his slit throat contorting and jagged, added to the nightmare.

Gil's stern command, "Wait here," was a feeble attempt to assert control in a place incapable of reason. With that, he left the women and a semi-conscious Marty in the shadowy tunnel, plunging into the unknown.

Gil heard splashing behind him. A hand landed on his shoulder and held him in place. It was Angelica. She said, "You paid for muscle. It's time we earned our keep." She pushed Gil behind her. Leah moved into place between them. Gil looked back into the tunnel. Marty leaned against the rough stone wall and was rubbing his injured temple with his finger tips. Angelica said, "Go wait with Marty. We shouldn't be too long."

Gil tried to object. "I don't think you understand the gravity of the situation." He knew he didn't understand it, so how could they.

The buzzing increased in volume and intensity and pierced the confined space. Gil fell to his knees almost sinking beneath the bloody stream. He covered his ears with the palms of his hands. The piercing whine penetrated through every orifice on his body. He dragged himself out of the stream. Gil fell face first onto the floor. The pain was unbearable. He struggled to stay conscious. His vision blurred as he was overwhelmed by the pain.

Angelica and Leah cautiously approached the five figures that in response, turned their attention to them. Jimmy gratefully resumed working on the door. The cloud figures now seemed uninterested in him.

Basic stepped forward to meet the attacking women. When he did that, the buzzing stopped. The chamber was bathed in blessed silence. Gil's ears rang, but he was no longer in intense pain. He looked up. The warrior women reached the line of disfigured figures.

Leah swung her Louisville slugger at Number One. Her expectation was that she would connect and she prepared for the impact to run up the length of the bat. But her swing passed through the figure of Number One and threw her off balance. The cloud just parted and the bat passed through. Then the cloud reconfigured itself back into Number One. Gil heard a single word escape from her lips. "Shit."

Angelica swung both the bat and her machete, one in each hand, like some kind of Samurai warrior out of a Manga story book. The cloud-men broke apart at each stroke and reconfigured. She alternated swinging the bat and machete to no avail.

The figures didn't retaliate. They flanked the women. Angelica and Leah ended up fighting back-to-back, striking at these hideous manifestations to no ill effect.

In the middle of the chaos, Jimmy's triumphant cheer echoed through the chamber, a battle cry as he wielded the obsidian key, breaking through the lock. In response, the ghost-like cloud-men underwent a sinister transformation. The door creaked open, the figures expanded and an ominous buzzing filled the air once more.

Undaunted, Jimmy pressed forward, moving beyond the doorway. Gil dropped to his knees, clutching his ears as the buzzing reached brain-piercing intensity, once again. Something beyond explanation was happening to the cloud figures. It appeared as if the clouds were metamorphizing into a myriad of insects. Every variety of biting, stinging, boring and blood-sucking thing was represented.

Leah and Angelica became engulfed by the swirling cloud entities, their agonized screams becoming the final overture to their failed assault.

The women thrashed and screamed as the clouds hungrily tore at their flesh. Gil looked up from his feeble hiding spot, witnessing the grotesque transformation of the clouds. Tens of thousands of living things, each intent on destruction, tore pieces from the women and carried them away, a grotesque scavenging multitude.

Leah tossed her bat, frantically swatting at the relentless horde of insects feasting upon her. Angelica, her bat abandoned but desperately clutching her machete, flailed her arms at the oncoming swarm, her exposed skin writhing with the relentless carnivores.

A brutal accident occurred as her machete swung too wide, striking Leah in the midriff. Amid the confusion and noise, the women's screams mingled with the infernal buzzing.

Gil rose to his feet, casting a desperate glance back towards the tunnel, where Marty still leaned against the wall, muttering incoherently, his ears firmly sealed against the piercing onslaught with the palms of both hands. Returning his gaze to the horrifying exhibition near the door, Gil bore witness to the women's excruciating demise.

Leah was reduced to a nightmarish vision, on her knees, her arms stripped of flesh, revealing gnarled bone and sinew. The insect cloud continued its relentless assault, erasing her facial features.

Meanwhile, Angelica, one knee touching the floor, had one arm ravaged to the bone, was swinging her machete with the other, her face contorted in pain.

The relentless insects closed in on Angelica, obscuring her form until it was indistinguishable from the swarm itself. In a chilling transformation, a segment of the swarm formed into a semblance of Basic, a grotesque parody of the man.

Drawing closer to Gil, Basic was flanked by the intensifying swarm, which continued to strip away the last scraps of flesh from the two women.

Unexpectedly, the entire swarm, except for Basic, dissolved into the darkness of the cavern. All that remained were the discarded bats and machete, alongside the glistening skeletons, illuminated dimly by the glow of the headlamps still attached to their naked skulls.

Jimmy reappeared in the doorway. His laughter was tinged with childlike glee as he held aloft two handfuls of gleaming gold nuggets. "It's here!" he cried, jubilant. "It's all right here. It's real, Gil. It's fucking real!" His proclamation echoed down the dark tunnel.

Gil felt an eerie, momentary connection with Basic. The entity seemed to convey a malevolent amusement, it almost smiled. It could have been an illusion, an effect of the dim light and wavering headlamp beams. The swarm of insects turned inward, focusing on Jimmy.

Basic, floating just inches above the floor, drifted closer to Jimmy. As the swarm drew near, Jimmy extended his gold-filled hands toward it. The horror that had befallen the others in the crypt had eluded him. Basic's hand brushed the gold, and Jimmy's smile wavered.

He spoke to Basic as if it were sentient, "Can you believe this? And there's so much more inside."

Basic's hand stopped caressing the gold and engulfed Jimmy's hand. Panic welled up in Jimmy's eyes as he struggled in vain to free his hand. He dropped the gold nuggets in his free hand and attempted to strike Basic, but his fist passed through the entity's head and torso without effect. Remarkably, Basic maintained its grip, preventing Jimmy from falling to the ground. There was something tangible to this disgusting thing, a revelation that sent shivers down Gil's spine.

The Basic cloud figure began to change. From where it connected with Jimmy's hand within its, the myriad of insects returned. They creeped up his arm. Jimmy's transformation was grotesque. The phantom's extremities embraced him, limb by limb, while Gil watched in a numbing trance. The swarm advanced, unrelenting, across Jimmy's body. His face contorted with a combination of panic and bewilderment, a macabre display of fear that Gil had witnessed countless times in the last ten minutes.

The chittering circle of bugs tightened its grip, and Jimmy's scream pierced the chamber. Gradually, the bugs eclipsed his face, obliterating his eyes and nose, leaving only his mouth. A solitary word escaped his trembling lips in a desperate plea: "Mommy." Then, an eerie silence descended as the insects washed over, and into, his open mouth.

Jimmy, encased in the writhing cocoon, stood upon the threshold of the gold room. His headlamp the only vestige of humanity. The swarm's writhing, chaotic dance concealed his fate, until, in an abrupt departure, the insects dispersed. All that remained was Jimmy's skeletal frame, stripped bare, save for the stubbornly glowing headlamp, revealing a few glistening gold nuggets on the ground.

Gil waded through the blood-slick stream back to his friend. "Come on, buddy. Let's get out of here."

Marty regarded Gil with an alien gaze. "My head's pounding."

"I know. You'll be fine. Let's go."

Marty's voice quivered with uncertainty. "Didn't Leah come with us?"

"Yeah, Leah and Angelica were with us."

Marty seemed puzzled. "Where are they now?"

Gil decided the brutal truth could come later. "They've already left. They're waiting for us up top."

Marty's brows furrowed. "Up top? Where are we, kiddo? It's dark and it stinks here."

"I know. Let's go."

Marty's legs seemed to fail him as he collapsed into Gil's arms, but the bloody stream offered some buoyancy. They waded on, and after a hundred yards, Marty regained control of his legs, walking unassisted.

The ascent up the spiral staircase, now saturated with blood, proved a grueling challenge. Gil's clothing weighed him down, and every precarious step spelled potential disaster. They paused to catch their breath every few steps.

Close to one in the morning, they reached the base of the rope ladder in the first chamber. Gil fell to his knees, utterly drained. He marveled at Marty, who, despite being two decades older, remained steadfast. Marty patted Gil on the shoulder, then resolutely placed his foot on the ladder's first rung. "Don't give up now, kid, or we'll be stuck down here forever."

Marty strained with each ascent, hand over hand, one rung at a time. Gil, too, clung to the ladder, waiting for Marty to get ahead, his breaths heavy with exhaustion. When Marty's feet passed the lower reaches of the landfill, Gil began his own climb, determined to escape this nightmarish descent into hell.

Gil slouched in his chair; weariness etched into every line of his body. With a lazy movement, he extended a foot to nudge Marty in the shoulder, who reluctantly roused himself from the floor and fell back into the oversized easy chair. Both men were caked in filth and gripped by exhaustion. Right now, a shower was more desirable than eighty million dollars in gold. Marty's head lolled back against the chair, and Gil strained to ease the tension in his neck, swaying his head from side to side.

Stretching his leg forward, Gil tapped Marty's knee with his toe, prompting Marty to crack open one eye and silently query him with a raised chin.

Gil closed his eyes and dragged his hand across his grizzled face, releasing a sigh before uttering, "We have to go back, you know."

Marty's eye closed, and he waved a dismissively limp hand from his chair. "No way."

Gil's voice grew resolute. "Yes, there's no other way."

"Why?" Marty inquired.

"Because I won't abandon eighty million dollars in that fucking hole. Is that reason enough for you?"

Marty remained mute, his breathing steady and deep, falling into the embrace of sleep within the armchair. Gil's head bobbed, fighting to stay conscious just long enough to get to the longed-for shower. He staggered to his feet, traversed the hallway to his room, while Marty snorted and turned in his chair, plunging into REM sleep.

Gil reappeared in the living room, clutching a blanket, which he carefully draped over Marty's sleeping form and tucked in the sides. He retreated to his room, found the shower, and entered fully clothed, the hot water cascading over his face, washing away the gruesome remnants of their descent. He leaned his head against the wall, whispering to the water, "We're going back. And then it'll be over."

Around noon, Marty awoke in the easy chair, greeted by the faint glow of daylight filtering through drawn blinds. He grimaced as he tried to stretch his aching neck, but panic soon seized him. His head wouldn't budge and his hands were trapped beneath the blanket. He struggled to stand but found himself fused to the chair. Frustration and exasperation welled up as he exclaimed, "Oh, for Christ's sake!"

The dried blood had glued him to the chair, and the blanket transformed into a straitjacket. Calling out to Gil proved futile, and Marty's struggles led to some cramping and an eventual breakthrough. He managed to free his right hand and commenced the arduous task of disentangling himself from the chair.

After a strenuous battle, Marty regained his footing. The chair and blanket were ruined and his clothing in shambles. He headed towards the hallway and the beckoning shower.

As he reached the living room's edge, with a rattle of keys, the apartment door creaked open, and Gil entered, bearing two sizable shopping bags from a local outdoor outfitter. He greeted Marty, saying, "Hey, I'm glad you're up. I got something for us when we go back."

Marty's disbelief was palpable. "Go back?" Marty swallowed hard. "Back where? Not to the crypt?"

Gil nodded and smiled. "Yes, the crypt. I told you. I'm not leaving anything down there. So, we're going back."

Marty hung his head, leaning on the hallway wall for support, his voice laden with defeat. "Fine. What's in the bags?"

Gil dropped one of the bags and reached into the other, revealing a green mass of rubber with attached boots. "I got us hip waders."

---

## THE CRYPT

## AGAIN

"Did you bring that Latin thing?" Gil inquired in a hushed tone as they descended the rope ladder into the abyss.

"What Latin thing? The dictionary? Yeah, I brought it." When they reached the bottom of the ladder, Marty rifled through his satchel, retrieving the worn dictionary for Gil.

Marty secured his satchel within the confines of his over-sized hip waders and sweated profusely, the unyielding waders adding weight and discomfort. Gil, on the other hand, seemed impervious to the discomfort. Marty decided to suffer in silence.

Gil, ever the zealous scholar, flipped through the pages of the dictionary, his gaze oscillating between the inscriptions on the chamber's wall and the book in his hands. "Ah, there it is. 'DESCENDIT.' You see that? It says that right there on the wall."

Marty cautiously approached the carvings pointed out by Gil, who prevented him from tumbling into the same hole into which Basic had disappeared. Chiseled into the rock were two words: DESCENDIT and below that DOLOR, just above the ominous hole.

Gil enunciated the definition of the first word, "It says here that Descendit means 'to go down.'" He continued to search and soon uncovered the meaning of the second word. "And Dolor means 'pain' or 'distress'. Go down and pain. Well, that's what it was, I guess. Basic definitely went down, and it sounded painful."

Gil shook his head in disbelief. "What the hell? Was that a warning about the hole? Hard to decipher this Fernando guy, you know what I mean."

Gil led Marty to the entrance of the caverns, where he pointed out the Latin inscriptions etched into the rock above the entrance: "VADE RETRO SATANA." Marty clambered up a small ledge and ran his fingers over the engraved words as Gil delved into the dictionary.

Gil soon found what he was searching for and shared his findings, saying, "Well, I suppose we know what the 'Satana' part implies without checking, but it's reassuring to have it confirmed. Devil, Satan, and all that. 'Vade' and 'Retro' mean 'Go Back.' 'Go back Satan'? Or perhaps it's a warning, like 'go back, Satan is here'? Latin doesn't seem as straightforward as one might hope."

Marty, finding solace in the beauty of the etched letters, commented, "It's pretty, though."

Gil looked at Marty with bewilderment, to which Marty hastily clarified, "I mean, it would be aesthetically pleasing under different circumstances."

"Right. Pretty," Gil replied. "Are we in the same room? Come on, I've got to show you what this meat grinder looks like."

Marty followed Gil into the next chamber, their headlamp beams played along the walls and ceiling. Gil recounted the harrowing experience of losing Basic and others in this labyrinth. "We lost Basic back there, down that frigging hole. We made it to here, and then we lost Arbuckle and that Stretch kid. I swear, it was one of the most painful things I've ever witnessed. Stretch was doing fine, walking on those logs, but then he tripped on a piece of rock embedded in the wood, and he tumbled. Once that log started rolling, it was all over. Arbuckle rushed out to save his friend, and they both got run through this thing like a meat grinder. It was horrible."

Marty cast his headlamp's feeble light across the modified bridge and asked, "Didn't you do anything?"

"What could I do? This contraption ate them. It happened so fast. I really thought Stretch would make it across."

"So that's why all the lumber on the next trip."

"Exactly. And now it's as safe as it can be. Come on," Gil urged.

Gil led the way across the modified bridge, and Marty stopped halfway to peer over the side, the weak headlamp-beam unable to penetrate the depths of the ravine. He shook his head and resumed crossing.

Gil consulted the dictionary once more, finding the definition for the word etched above the next doorway:

OBTERO. "That means to cut in two," he murmured, a tinge of frustration in his voice. "God damn it."

Marty inquired, "What's wrong?"

Gil returned the dictionary to Marty, sighing, "I was too quick to kill Abaddon, as you pointed out, and I can't help but agree. But I was equally hasty in attempting to decipher this puzzle. I should have gathered the definitions before sending these people to their doom. They were getting paid to take risks, but we had no idea of the actual dangers."

Marty consoled his friend by patting him on the back, saying, "Yeah, you're an idiot, kiddo," before crab-crawling under the door and towards the next chamber.

Gil took slight offense but inquired, "And?"

Marty chuckled and retorted, "And nothing. You've always been impulsive. It makes you seem like an idiot. All these casualties? Your responsibility. So, yeah, you're an idiot. Nothing personal," Marty concluded, turning and walking away.

Gil lingered in the chamber for a moment while Marty advanced to the head of the stairway. He watched Marty's headlamp beam traverse the chamber's walls, vanishing from sight. Once the beam was no longer visible, Gil extinguished his own headlamp, enveloping himself in darkness.

Every word Marty said rang true. Gil's life had not always been marked by cold, calculated decisions, but he had grown accustomed to the thrill of living without consequence, taking what ever he desired. He was beholden to no one, accountable to nothing. He muttered to himself, "Screw Marty and his guilt trips," then flicked his headlamp back on and descended the staircase cautiously, his awkward hip waders a constant reminder of his imprudent actions. "I hope Marty breaks his god-damned neck," Gil fantasized quietly.

Marty waited for Gil to join him at the bottom of the stairs. Together, they waded through the eerie tunnel, the crimson stream now less deep and thus less taxing to navigate. Gil couldn't help but wonder about the source of all this blood.

Upon reaching the raised area in the next chamber, they halted and surveyed the surroundings. Leah, Angelica's, and Jimmy's skeletons remained undisturbed, exactly where they had fallen. Something stirred among the bones, but it was too far to make anything out.

Gil ascended the rise, while Marty remained behind, vigilant. The beam of Marty's headlamp darted around the space, eventually settling on a peculiar sight. A crimson centipede, its mandibles razor-sharp, slithered out of a crevice, traversed a section of the wall, and vanished into another hole. Smaller beetles and worms writhed on the surface of the wall. Marty unwittingly drew his face closer to the grotesque spectacle, only to recoil with a jerk, retreating to where Gil had left him.

From a few feet away, Gil observed the scene and inquired, "Everything okay?"

Marty's shoulders quivered as he responded, "Gives me the Willies."

Gil sought clarification, "What?"

"Those damn bugs," Marty whispered, his voice trembling. "Did you see the size of that centipede?"

"Centipede? I thought I was looking at a miniature train set. That thing was huge," Gil remarked, clearly shaken by the encounter.

Marty, fed up with their present circumstances, urged, "Go. Let's get this thing done." He gestured for Gil to move forward; an underlying anxiety etched across his face. "Go on, kiddo. I don't know how much more I have left in the tank."

Gil nodded, offering a reassuring wink before venturing toward the skeletal remains. The chamber remained eerily still, save for the rustling of exoskeletons as countless carrion-eating insects scuttled and clicked their way through the darkness. Among the bones on the floor, there was no single entity but a collection of grotesque creatures. A massive red centipede commanded attention, encircled by orange-and-black beetles that glistened like sharkskin under Gil's headlamp beam.

The centipede Marty had encountered in the tunnel now seemed a mere dwarf compared to the colossal specimen Gil observed, curling up within Angelica's ribcage. This creature, the size of a small dog, sprawled out at three feet long.

Leah and Angelica's skeletons were stripped of flesh, muscle, and sinew, save for a solitary belt buckle where Leah's waist once had been. Gil picked it up, thinking that Marty might appreciate the sentiment.

Gil shifted his focus to Jimmy's remains, which had similarly lost all soft matter. Despite this, the bones remained moist, catching the light from his headlamp. He swept the light over Jimmy's skeletal frame, discovering several thumb-nail-sized gold nuggets beneath the body. He examined one, contemplating its modern-day worth, possibly hundreds of dollars. Dozens more nuggets lay strewn at Jimmy's feet.

As Gil gathered these precious finds, he uncovered the obsidian key nestled among the gold. It seemed impervious to the ravages of insects. He held it, watching the light dance upon its surface, noting its simplicity with subtle scrollwork at the head. He stashed the key in his pocket, for posterity.

Gil beckoned Marty, shouting, "It seems safe here now. No boogie men to speak of. "

Marty, ever vigilant, queried, "Any snakes?"

Gil, incredulous, retorted, "Snakes? Centipedes as long as your leg, and now you worry about snakes?"

Marty's tone darkened, "I don't like snakes, kiddo."

They both approached the skeletons, and Gil passed Leah's belt buckle to Marty, who rubbed it thoughtfully, confessing, "I liked Leah."

"I know," Gil replied.

Marty, however, surprised Gil by tossing the belt buckle deep into the darkness. Puzzled, Gil said, "Hey," aiming his headlamp toward the buckle's landing point.

Gil gestured toward something lying in the distance, about thirty feet away, piled against the wall. Marty, peering through the shadows, questioned, "What do you make of that?"

Gil pointed, his voice heavy with dread, "You think maybe it's more bones?"

Marty, moving toward the pile, illuminated its grisly contents. These bones, although similarly stripped clean, bore evidence of a much greater violence. Some skulls were so crushed that they appeared fused, while rib cages and limbs were mutilated. Among the pile of remains lay remnants of sandwich wrappers and discarded water bottles, a stark contrast to the gold nuggets.

Gil, frustration mounting, muttered, "Oh, for fucks sake." Gil extended his headlamp's reach into the darkness, admitting, "You know what this is?"

Marty turned his gaze back to the pile of bones, then upward again. "No, what is it?"

"This is Basic, Stretch, Arbuckle, and the Number One and Two guys, all mixed together."

"Oh, shit! Are you serious?"

"Yeah. That's my lunch wrapper that day we ate near the rope ladder. We probably could have just dropped a rope ladder down that hole Basic fell in and ended up here. God damn it."

Gil nodded grimly, while Marty, laughing, remarked, "Yeah, this is hilarious."

"You are a sick, sick man."

"Me?" Marty was indignant, but smiling. He shook his head. "Gil, kiddo, this is too funny not to laugh. If I don't laugh, I might as well die right here." Marty kept laughing as he walked back to Jimmy's body.

Gil, meanwhile, kicked at a plastic water bottle, disturbing another giant, scarlet centipede. He joined Marty at Jimmy's side, lifting an eyebrow and holding up the obsidian key for Marty to see.

Marty, puzzled, asked, "Where did you find that?"

"Jimmy had it," Gil replied, dropping the key into his satchel. With renewed determination, he urged, "Let's go. There's money to be had."

The duo crossed into the next room through the doorway Jimmy, an unlikely locksmith, had opened. The chamber revealed a low ceiling but a vast expanse. Gil's headlamp's feeble light barely reached the distant walls, unveiling a small mound of gold nuggets, disappointingly smaller than anticipated. The pile contained maybe fifty or sixty pounds of gold, far from the promised fortune.

Gil, frustrated, shook his head. "I knew it was all bullshit. Didn't I tell you it was all lies?"

Marty, refusing to surrender hope, suggested, "Let's take a look around before we rush to judgement. This cave is pretty big."

Gil, grumbling, began collecting the gold nuggets into a cloth sack. "Fifty pounds is still worth something. It may not be eighty million, but it could be close to a million. That lying shit."

Marty, unperturbed, ventured ahead. As he kicked a stray nugget toward the pile, his headlamp revealed another doorway. "Hey, there's something over here."

Gil, dejected, muttered, "Oh, no." He turned to Marty, questioning, "What are you looking at?"

Marty, certain of what he'd seen, affirmed, "It's another door. What should we do?"

Gil, bracing for disappointment, sighed, "I'm coming." His exasperation and fatigue were evident in his tone of voice. He joined Marty near the doorway. "Wait here."

Marty, a touch too quickly, said, "Of course. This is your expedition, after all."

Gil shrugged the sarcasm off. "Thanks. I'll see what's what." He turned as if struck by a thought, adding, "If anything happens to me, there's a sack of gold nuggets back there. Don't blow it all in one place."

Marty grinned. "Well, here's hoping then."

Gil stopped abruptly, looking back, his headlamp blinding Marty momentarily. Marty shielded his eyes with his hand. Gil muttered under his breath, "Such a dick. Such a dick. Remind me again, why are we friends?"

Marty shrugged and replied, "I think I've just always felt sorry for you."

Gil turned back toward the door. "Hm. I thought that was me feeling sorry for you."

Marty chuckled. "I've seen stronger relationships based on less than mutual pity. Go on, kiddo. Take a walk in the dark and tell me what you see in there."

Gil said nothing and ventured into the passage. As he progressed, the tunnel quickly narrowed, and after about twenty feet, he spotted the other door. Gil shouted back at Marty, "There is another door, man. Jesus Christ."

"Be careful. These doors haven't been very lucky for anyone opening them."

Gil examined it meticulously. It stood seven feet high and three feet wide, crafted from hickory beams soaked in creosote, much like the one that had gruesomely claimed the lives of One and Two. His headlamp's beam swept across the door, revealing no notches in the stone doorframe. He checked the ceiling for potential traps and the floor for hidden mechanisms, finding nothing. Finally, he focused his attention on the door itself.

His fingers ran up and down the wood's surface, searching for any triggers or traps. Two horizontal metal bands held the door together with heavy bolts, and there were no handles or rings. Between the metal bands was a single keyhole, barely visible in the darkness.

Gil muttered to himself, "I wish I'd been this careful from the beginning. Might have saved a life or two. Or five. Or eight." His fingers found some notches at the top of the stone border, and etched into the stone, he saw the word "DESPERATO."

Gil called out to Marty, "Hey. You got that dictionary handy?"

Marty's voice came from right behind him, startling Gil. "Jesus-fucking-Christ. You scared the shit out of me. I thought you were going to wait back in the cave?"

Marty retrieved the Latin dictionary from his satchel. "I got lonely. Sue me." He found the word "Desperato" and mumbled something Gil couldn't hear.

Gil insisted, "Out loud, please. Jesus."

Marty glanced up from the dictionary. "You're not going to like it, kiddo."

"Why? Give me the bad news first, doc."

Marty returned to the dictionary. "Desperato, means hopeless."

Gil stepped back, a sense of foreboding washing over him. He rubbed his chin with a gloved hand, deep in thought. "Marty?"

Marty, using his friend's first name to underscore the gravity of the situation, replied, "Yes, Gil?"

"There's a keyhole in this door."

"And?"

"And I'm wondering if I'm so curious that I need to open that door."

"And?"

"I might be. And you know what that makes me?"

"Do tell?"

Gil rocked his head back and forth, attempting to dispel the mounting stress. "I think that makes me hopeless."

Marty nodded, understanding the gravity of the situation. "Ah. So, you think the word above the door is specifically intended for you?"

Gil's headlamp illuminated Marty's face as he responded, "Could be."

Gil approached the door, pushing against it with all his strength, but it didn't budge. Marty joined him, but the door remained immovable. "As expected," Gil muttered, sharing a knowing look with Marty.

Gil retrieved his lock-picking tools from his satchel, selecting a prong and a probe. He inserted them into the keyhole, attempting to identify any tumblers or gears inside. The lock appeared to be more complex than he initially thought, a testament to the craftsmanship of fifteenth-century lock-makers.

After several attempts, Gil gave a frustrated sigh and contemplated his next move. Marty asked, "Hey, kiddo?"

Gil, still focused on the lock, replied, "What?"

"Did you pick up that stone key that Jimmy had at that other door?"

Gil gave Marty a skeptical look. "Yeah. I did. So?"

Marty suggested, "Why don't you try that?"

"Another frigging genius-move. Of course."

It hadn't crossed Gil's mind to use the obsidian key, assuming it was only meant for the first door. He rummaged through his bag, eventually retrieving the key. Holding it up to his headlamp's beam, he noticed it shared the same material as the lock's faceplate. Gil then handed the key to Marty. "Here. Your idea. You should have the honor."

Marty took the key, and they both stood before the door. Marty's hands trembled as he inserted the obsidian key into the lock. It turned with a barely audible click as a tumbler met a gear. He turned the key another quarter turn, and another click confirmed progress.

Excitement filled Marty's voice. "It's working."
However, when he tried to withdraw the key, he found that his hand was stuck to it. Panic set in as he struggled to free his hand. "Gil? Gil, something's wrong."

Gil watched in horror as Marty's hand and arm started to change, becoming as black and glittery as the obsidian key. Marty cried out, "Get it off me. It hurts."

Gil stepped back, unable to comprehend the surreal scene unfolding before him. Marty's transformation continued, the blackness engulfing him, leaving only his eyes rolling around in anguish.

Unable to bear the sight any longer, Gil reached for a small rock-hammer from his bag. He struck Marty's wrist, causing his hand to shatter, and his friend's transformed body fell to the ground. The door crept open slightly.

As the realization hit Gil that the door was linked to the key and Marty, he was left with a mix of emotions – fear, anger, relief. After a moment of contemplation, he distanced himself from Marty's body, unwilling to risk the same fate. Finally, with the door ajar, he wondered what other mysteries and challenges lay behind it. Using the hammer head, to avoid any contact with the door, he pushed it open.

A rush of putrid air surged through the opening in the doorway, assaulting Gil's senses with a horrible stench, akin to the rotting remnants of a dozen corpses. The atmosphere clung to his skin, clammy and unsettling, leaving him to wonder whether he had just inhaled an unseen evil that might linger, or a silent assassin poised to strike him down in the future.

Desperation masked as curiosity, Gil tugged at his shirt collar, a futile defense against the unrelenting olfactory assault. He recalled a distant, obscure factoid that all smells were particulate, a chilling reminder that what he detected in the air could be seeping into the recesses of his very being, an unwelcome bringer of disease or pain.

Hunched in a low-ceilinged tunnel, Gil navigated the labyrinth, the flickering beam of his headlamp casting uncertain shadows. A right turn beckoned, and as the tunnel expanded, he could finally stand upright, albeit with a sense of caution that weighed heavily on his shoulders.

Recollections of the ominous word "DESPERATO" clung to his thoughts, its meaning shrouded in ambiguity. Was Marty's gruesome death the hopelessness foretold by that cryptic inscription? Gil moved forward, hesitating at the right turn, his headlamp spilling forth a blinding gleam as it met the polished gold that adorned the chamber's walls.

Blinded temporarily, he retreated to the tunnel's safety, gasping for composure. He ventured forth once more, this time with eyes squinting against the golden radiance. What he beheld was a sight to stun the bravest of souls: the walls adorned with an opulent tapestry of gold, a wealth beyond reckoning. Gil picked up a small golden medallion etched with images of a dancer and birds. He placed it gingerly back on the wall.

A wooden box, long and eerie in its resemblance to a coffin, lay at the base of one gilded wall. Its material mirrored that of the chamber's doors, soaked in creosote to defy the ravages of time. Gil's trembling hands traced the surface, smooth and oddly warm, and then it came, a muffled thud, a haunting heartbeat from within the box.

Gil fell onto his backside as he scrambled to escape whatever horror might be contained in that box. He crab-crawled backwards. He peered left and right, the gold glinted, his headlamp beams exposed figurines and animals, collars and necklaces.

The lid from the box raised and dropped back with a bang. Gil screamed. His heart raced in fear. He scrambled backwards again, unable to take his eyes off the box. His backwards motion was impeded when something placed a foot on his back. He screamed again. The lid of the box raised. This time it toppled into the space between the box and the wall. A small, golden statue of a bird with emerald eyes dropped to the floor as the lid fell.

Gil looked back to see what was preventing his escape. It was indeed a foot, attached to a leg. Gil scrambled to his feet and found himself staring into the face of Dante. But Dante was dead! He was certain he'd killed the man back at the mansion.

A laugh came from behind Gil and he spun at the sound. Sitting up in the creosote-soaked-box was Fenriz Abaddon. Gil shouted, "Fenriz? How?" He fell to his knees.

Dante stepped around Gil to assist his Master. Abaddon slithered out of the casket. "How do you like my little collection now, Gil?"

Gil's world crumbled, and his hysterical laughter became a discordant symphony of madness, teetering on a knife's edge of reason. Tears streamed down his cheeks, and the fabric of reality unraveled before him.

Dante and Abaddon watched, silent sentinels to the unraveling mind, until the laughter dissolved into whimpering. Abaddon leaned in, their faces mere inches apart, and posed a riddle, "What was that last word etched into the wall?"

Gil, among the remnants of his shattered sanity, pondered the word 'hopeless.' A glimmer of comprehension flickered in his eyes, and he whispered, "Doomed."

Abaddon grinned, and in that singular word, destiny took a terrifying twist. "Still an unbeliever?"

Before Gil could respond, Dante rendered him unconscious with one well placed blow to the side of his head.

When Gil regained awareness, he found himself trussed at the ankles and with his arms pinioned behind his back. Attempts to right himself in the tight confines only made his position worse. Creosote permeated the wood. His throat constricted with each breath.

Dante's face moved into his range of vision. "Oh good," he chuckled, "you're awake." Dante's face moved out of field and then reappeared. "I wouldn't want you to sleep through this part." Dante raised the lid and laid it along the edge of the coffin. "Enjoy the gold. It's all yours."

In concert with the hammer blows, Gil's screams died in the dark.

### The end

# DISCLAIMER:

This is an original story, written in its entirety by me,
a human being. The storyline, situations and
characters were created by me. I wrote the story all
by myself, from beginning to end.

I did use ChatGPT 3.5 to edit and proofread for
spelling, syntax, grammar and punctuation. I used it
as any other proofreading or editing app
(Grammarly, Quillbot) might be used.

I used the free version. It only allowed me to process
three pages at a time. I don't know if a similar
restriction exists in the paid version.

ChatGPT 3.5 did not change any of the story, nor did
it create or suggest any additional scenarios that were
not in the original draft.

I hope that you enjoyed the tale.

Sincerely

M.R. Whittaker

Manufactured by Amazon.ca
Bolton, ON

41005219R00131